Guardian and the *Observer* on publication, and THE
DAY I WAS ERASED was Children's Book of the Week
in the *Times*.

C334441969

Also by Lisa Thompson:

"*A great cast of characters and an intriguing mystery – I loved it!*"
Ross Welford, bestselling author of Time Travelling with a Hamster

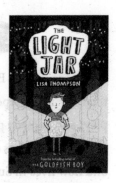

"*Pure, breathtaking genius*"
Max Evans, bestselling author of who Let the Gods Out

"*Brimming with Thompson's characteristic warmth and wisdom*"
The Bookseller

LISA THOMPSON

THE BOY WHO FOOLED THE WORLD

SCHOLASTIC

For my agent, Adam.

Published in the UK by Scholastic Children's Books, 2020
Euston House, 24 Eversholt Street, London, NW1 1DB, UK
A division of Scholastic Limited.

London – New York – Toronto – Sydney – Auckland
Mexico City – New Delhi – Hong Kong

Text © Lisa Thompson, 2020

The right of Lisa Thompson to be identified as the author
of this work has been asserted by them under the
Copyright, Designs and Patents Act 1988.

ISBN 978 1407 18513 2

A CIP catalogue record for this book
is available from the British Library.

Printed by CPI Group (UK) Ltd, Croydon, CR0 4YY
Papers used by Scholastic Children's Books are made
from wood grown in sustainable forests.

1 3 5 7 9 10 8 6 4 2

This is a work of fiction. Names, characters, places, incidents
and dialogues are products of the author's imagination or are used
fictitiously. Any resemblance to actual people, living or dead,
events or locales is entirely coincidental.

www.scholastic.co.uk

CHAPTER ONE

Tidying the Art Cupboard

My best friend, Mason Ferguson, had a plastic bucket on his head.

He'd found it on a shelf in Mrs Frampton's art cupboard and decided to put it on and do a silly dance. The bucket began to slip and wobble.

"Look. At. Me. Cole. I. Am. A. Robot," he said. He accidentally banged his head against the wall and gave a loud, echoing "ooompfff" from inside the bucket. Normally this would have made me crack up, but I wasn't in the mood for joking around. Mason took it off his head and sighed.

"Do you think everyone else is there yet?" he said as I sorted through a box of glue sticks, taking out

1

the dried-up ones with no lids and throwing them away.

"Yeah," I said, with a huff. "They're probably having ice cream for breakfast."

Two coaches had been booked to arrive at school an hour before registration, and by the time we'd made it in, the rest of our year had left on the trip to Thrill Kingdom. Our form tutor said that instead of lessons, Mason and I were going to spend the day helping to get the school ready for a very important visitor who was coming tomorrow. Tidying the art cupboard was our first task.

"I bet they go on Dragon's Hollow first before it gets too busy," said Mason, staring at a big bag of clay.

"Yeah, I would," I said. "Niall told me he was going to go on it at least ten times."

Mason sighed again. Dragon's Hollow was famous for being the best and fastest ride at Thrill Kingdom, and everyone in year seven was going to go on it, except for us. The whole of the year had been given a letter about the amusement park trip on the first day of term. I had left mine on the kitchen table, even though I knew there was no way my parents would be able to afford the ticket price. The letter was never mentioned and no one at school was surprised

I wasn't going. I'd only been at Crowther High a short while, but thanks to Leyton Morgan and Niall Wright I was already known as "Poor Kid Cole", which was supposed to be a riff on Old King Cole from the nursery rhyme but just sounded stupid. I really, *really* hoped that the two of them threw up all over Dragon's Hollow.

Mason kicked at a box of paper on the floor.

"I can't believe we're missing out. It's so unfair," he said. His parents had tons of money so they could easily pay for him to go, but they hadn't signed the form in time. They both had really busy jobs and weren't around much. Sometimes I think they forgot he existed.

"How are you two getting on?" asked Mrs Frampton, poking her head around the cupboard door. "Oh, what an improvement!"

"I don't get it, Miss," said Mason. "Why are we tidying up a *cupboard*?"

Mrs Frampton picked up the bucket that Mason had put on his head, moved it to a different shelf, studied it carefully for a moment, then moved it back again.

"The whole of the art department must look the best it can for our special guest, Mason," she said.

"Marika Loft is a very, *very* important artist and her visit could have a real impact on our school."

Marika Loft was a famous painter who had been a pupil at Crowther High about twenty years ago. I say famous – most of us had barely heard of her – but we all knew that she had been on TV a lot and was really rich. Her paintings sold for thousands and thousands of pounds, and she had houses in London, Paris and New York. It was apparently quite a big deal to have a real-life celebrity coming to see us.

"Mr Taylor has asked if you can pin these up in the corridors. Somewhere nice and obvious so that all pupils can read it," said Mrs Frampton. She passed me some A4 sheets of paper and gave Mason a box of drawing pins. I took a look.

MARIKA LOFT VISIT

School Rules

FAMOUS artist, VIP and former pupil Marika Loft will soon be visiting our school. Please abide by the following rules, and let's REMIND her WHAT A SPECIAL PLACE Crowther High is!

1) All pupils should be on their best behaviour
   at ALL times.
2) DO NOT approach Marika or speak to her
   unless she speaks to you first.
3) If Marika does speak to you then you must
   reply in a polite, friendly manner. Use your
   best voice.
4) Do not stare. Famous people do not like
   BEING STARED at.

"When you've finished with the posters, go to Mr Taylor's office and find out what he'd like you to do next," said Mrs Frampton. "You're doing a fabulous job, both of you. Well done!"

She was being extra nice: she must have felt sorry for us, stuck here while year seven spent the day riding on rollercoasters and eating chips. The thought of everyone running around Thrill Kingdom in the sunshine made me feel sick with envy.

"Come on, let's go and put these up," I said, waving the posters at Mason. We both huffed and headed to the corridor.

"Have you seen Marika Loft's paintings?" asked Mason, as we stopped by a notice board. "They're just pictures of coloured boxes. They're well weird." I held up a poster and he pushed a pin into each corner.

"Yeah, apparently each box represents something in her life depending on what colour it is," I said.

Mason snorted. "Anyone who pays thousands of pounds for a canvas covered in coloured squares must have more money than sense. She's probably laughing behind everyone's backs."

We moved on and pinned another poster to the back of a door.

"Is your party still happening? Won't everyone be late back from Thrill Kingdom?" I asked. It had been Mason's birthday at the weekend and his party was tonight.

"Yes! Five o'clock. You are still coming, aren't you? Don't forget, will you?" he said.

"Of course I won't forget," I said. "I wouldn't miss Thrill Kingdom *and* Mason Ferguson's party in one day, would I?" Mason smiled. We'd been mates for a while but this would be my first time seeing the inside of his house and I was quite excited about it. I'd never been invited round before. Apparently, it was absolutely massive and really posh. Even the party invitation looked expensive. It was gold-embossed and on really thick card.

I was worried about what someone who was that rich would expect for a present, so last Friday I'd asked Dean Grant what he was giving Mason. Dean just frowned at me.

"What party?" he'd grunted. "I don't know nothing about any party?" I'd just shrugged and told him not to worry about it. I didn't dare ask anyone else in case they hadn't been invited either. Mason was obviously asking a few select people and I didn't want to put my foot in it.

We put the rest of the posters up around the school and then made our way to Mr Taylor's office.

"What do you think he'll make us do next? Polish the stairs?" grumbled Mason. The door to his office was open and we could see Mr Taylor on the phone. He spotted us and beckoned us in.

"Of course ... of course, yes, yes..." he said to the person on the end of the phone. "We'll make sure we have plenty of turmeric tea and a platter of fruit... Yes, yes ... no citrus. I understand..."

He was frantically scribbling things down, his face bright red.

"And can I just say, Declan, that the school is *so* honoured that Ms Loft is taking time out of her extremely hectic schedule to come and see us. I know the pupils are *incredibly* excited about her visit."

Mason looked at me and raised his eyebrows. This was news to us.

"... and we hope that Marika, I mean Ms Loft, will appreciate that our art block is always ... um ... open to any sponsors ... um ... helping towards a refurbishment..."

At this point Mr Taylor went even redder.

"Of course, of course," he said, laughing nervously. "We look forward to welcoming her tomorrow. Goodbye!"

He hung up the phone.

"Boys!" he said, leaping out of his seat. "You've put up the posters, yes?"

We both nodded.

"Fantastic." He wiped a bead of sweat from his forehead and went over to a corner of the room where there were two large brooms. My heart sank.

"Now, as you know, tomorrow's visit from Marika Loft is *extremely* important to the school. We need to ensure that we make the *best* impression."

He took hold of the brooms and stood in front of us.

"I'd like you to sweep the path that leads from the main doors to the car park. Get rid of every stone and leaf."

I looked at Mason and he rolled his eyes as Mr Taylor passed him a broom.

"Off you go now." He rushed back to his desk. "You're doing a grand job. Really, really grand."

We turned and slowly made our way out of the office and across the foyer.

"Can you believe we missed Thrill Kingdom for this?" said Mason gloomily. We both sighed and walked towards the main doors, dragging the brooms behind us.

CHAPTER TWO

Mason's Birthday Party

Mason lived in an area called Woodlands Park, about a kilometre from the Sideway Estate where our house was. Last Christmas, Mum and Dad had taken us for a walk around Woodlands Park so that we could see the decorations outside the posh houses. One house was smothered with twinkling lights. It looked like a spider's web made of diamonds had been draped from the chimney down to the door. Another had nine life-sized mechanical reindeer on their front lawn – one with a shining red nose. Sometimes you could see inside the houses as well. I peered through one window at a tree so tall it reached the ceiling. My family dug the same plastic tree out of the loft every year, even though it was missing a few branches.

As we walked to Woodlands Park for Mason's birthday party, Dad pushed my little sister Mabel in her buggy. She'd refused to get buckled in, so we'd had a bit of a delay while Dad bribed her to sit still with the promise of a biscuit when they got home. Before we left I'd found a "Mega-Bouncy Ball" that I'd been given for my last birthday, still in its packaging. Dad wrapped it up for me and tried to make it look fancy by tying a purple ribbon around it. Mason was bound to have a mountain of presents from everyone else so, with any luck, I could hide my rubbish one at the back.

The further we walked away from our estate, the bigger the houses became. Mabel spotted a grand stone fountain in someone's front garden and we had to pause and stare at that for about three minutes.

"Don't keep stopping, Dad," I said. "I'm already late!"

"Look! Water goes splash, splash, splash!" said Mabel, brushing her blonde hair out of her eyes as she leant forward in the buggy.

"Come on, Mabel. We can have a look on the way back," said Dad, starting to walk. "We don't want Cole to miss any of the fun, do we?" Mabel slumped back into her buggy and pulled the blanket over her head in protest.

When we got to Mason's house I recognized it as the one that had been covered with the twinkly spider's web last Christmas. They had a large gravel driveway with enough room for about ten cars, and Dad had to drag Mabel's buggy backwards to get across the small stones. She still had her blanket over her head when Dad pressed the brass doorbell. When my sister got the hump, she was really good at sticking with it.

I couldn't hear any party sounds coming from inside. Everyone must be in the back garden. The door opened and Mason's parents greeted us with wide grins.

"Cole! Welcome!" said his mum. "I'm Tamara. We've heard so much about you, haven't we, Hugh?" Cole's dad nodded and flashed a set of white teeth at me. I grinned back. He was tanned and was wearing a blue shirt with smart suit trousers. He didn't look like the kind of man who wore jeans every day like my dad.

"Would you like to come in for a coffee?" said Hugh, looking Dad up and down.

"Thank you, but I'd better get back. Mabel is

getting grizzly and I promised her we could stop to see something on the walk home," said Dad. Mabel peeked out from behind the blanket then quickly hid her face again.

"Oh, yes," said Mason's mum. "You're not in Woodlands, are you?"

"No, but we're not far. We live on the Sideway Estate," said Dad.

The air around us seemed to chill a little.

I was itching to get inside but they were blocking the doorway and there was no sign of Mason yet. He was probably out the back with everybody else.

Hugh cleared his throat.

"I hear there's a really good mini-supermarket in the Sideway Estate. Opens all hours. Just when you need one!" he said.

Dad brightened.

"Yes, that's right! Though we don't tend to use it. It's quite expensive."

Everyone went silent again and Mason's mum checked her watch. Dad looked at me.

"Right, I should be on my way. I'll see you at seven then, Cole," he said. "Have a lovely time." Hugh moved out of the way and I stepped up into the house. Dad turned around and dragged Mabel's buggy back across the driveway, leaving two deep grooves in the gravel in his wake. I saw Mason's mum wince.

I looked around the hallway and tried not to gawp. It was the size of the entire ground floor of my house. There were several doors off to the left and right, and in the centre was a wide staircase. I peered up it to see a balcony and at least eight more doors leading off it. Everything was such a bright white, including the carpet, that I felt like I'd just stepped into heaven.

Hugh's mobile began to ring and he walked off into another room to answer it, closing the door behind him.

Tamara was staring down at my shoes. I quickly pulled them off and put them on a black tray that was just inside the front door.

"Are those socks fluffy?" she said, looking at my feet. I was wearing a pair of red socks covered in little jolly Santas, even though it was October. "What I mean is, does the red fluff come off easily?" I was about to say that I had no idea when Mason arrived, doing a massive skid across the carpet and nearly crashing right into me.

"Cole! You're here! I didn't hear the door. You all right?" he asked excitedly. I nodded, grinning. Tamara gave my feet one last stare before whispering something into Mason's ear, patting him on the shoulder and heading off to the back of the house.

"Happy birthday, Mason," I said, waving the wrapped-up Mega-Bouncy Ball at him. I looked around for a pile of presents so I could hide it with the others but couldn't see one.

"Thanks! I'll open it later," he said, putting it on the hall table next to a photograph of him with his mum and dad on a tropical beach. He opened the drawer of the table and took out what looked like two little blue plastic bags. He scrunched them up and threw them at me and they dropped to the floor.

"You'd better put those on," he said. I bent down and picked them up. They were shoe covers, like the ones you get at swimming pools. They looked a bit like shower caps with stretchy elastic around the edge. I saw that Mason was already wearing a pair over his socks. I stared at them for a bit, not quite sure why I had to wear them but thinking it was probably something to do with not getting fluff on the white carpet. Then I sat on the doormat and began to pull the plastic over my feet.

"They feel strange at first but they're brilliant for skidding in," said Mason. "I once managed to get from the study down to the cinema room in one go!"

I fiddled with the shoe covers. The house was so silent. Where was everybody?

"Is the coach back from Thrill Kingdom running late?" I asked. Mason scratched his head.

"Ah, right. Yeah, I was going to tell you... So, Mum and Dad said I could only have one friend over for my birthday and I picked you. It's just us, I'm afraid."

"Oh," I said.

I stood up. The blue plastic covers rustled against the soft, white carpet. This wasn't like any party that I'd ever been to before. Mason stared down, scuffing his wrapped foot against the floor so that it made a swishing sound.

"Hey, Mason," I said. "Did you just say you had a ... *cinema room*?" Mason slowly looked up at me and grinned.

"Come on," he said. "I'll show you around!"

Mason's house was incredible. Not only did it have a cinema room (with ten reclining chairs) but also a gaming room with loads of computer consoles, a gym (which looked, and smelt, like it had never been used) and a wine cellar (although we weren't allowed to go down there). When we got to an area he called "the den", which was like an extra lounge,

I got a chance to see the back garden. On the patio was a shiny basketball hoop, and beyond that a lawn that stretched on and on. The grass was as plush as the thick carpet indoors. To one side was a full-sized football goal.

"Wow, your garden is huge!" I said, not even trying to play it cool. "You've even got a goal! Can we play?"

"Ah, sorry, we can't. The lawn's just been treated," said Mason. I stared at the lush, green grass. It didn't look like anyone had ever trodden on it, let alone played football on it.

We went to his room next, which had a king-sized bed, a hammock and his own personal bathroom.

"You are sooo lucky," I said, thinking of my cold bedroom with the worn-out carpet and the mattress springs that dug into my ribs. I sat down on the hammock and swung back and forth. I would have given anything to live in a house like this. It was the most amazing place I'd ever been.

"Hang on! I haven't opened your present yet!" said Mason. I was about to tell him to wait until I'd gone home but he had already run off to get it. I cringed. He was surrounded by everything he could possibly want and now he was going to open the *only* present from his *only* party guest, and it was a pathetic one. I stayed on the hammock swinging slowly and then jumped as I heard a "WHOOP!" coming from downstairs. A few seconds later Mason appeared around his doorway.

"I've *always* wanted one of these!" he said, his eyes shining brightly. "Shall we try it out on the patio?"

"Um, OK!" I said, relieved that he seemed to like it.

I followed him downstairs and got my scruffy shoes from the tray by the door and, as if his life wasn't incredible enough, Mason appeared with a pair of bright white trainers.

"Are they XT50s?" I said, my mouth hanging open.

"Yeah, they were my birthday present from Mum and Dad," he said. "They're cool, aren't they?" I nodded as he passed me one to hold. I traced the toe with a finger. They were so bright they almost made my eyes water. XT50s were very, *very* expensive.

"They're amazing," I whispered, passing it back to him.

We headed to a big dining room with a wide glass door that looked out on to the patio and garden. Mason opened the door and we took the blue plastic covers off our feet and changed into our shoes.

Bouncing the ball on the patio was great fun. We

were laughing and shouting so much that his mum came out and told us to quieten down. Mason did one really huge bounce and I missed it and it landed in the middle of the immaculate lawn. He quickly ran across to get it, and his dad shouted out of the upstairs window for him to get off the grass.

"We'd better keep the bounces smaller," he said, going red. "We can keep it under control then."

We got to twenty-eight little bounces back and forth before his mum called us in for tea. We kicked our shoes off, put the plastic covers back over our socks and went inside.

Tea was pizza. We usually had frozen pizzas at home that had hardly any toppings on, but these ones had been delivered by a restaurant. On the boxes it read: *From Our Own Wood-Fired Pizza Oven*. I took three slices of one covered in pepperoni, some green-leafy stuff and red chillies. Tamara told me to help myself to a big wooden bowl full of salad but I just stuck with the pizza. I managed to eat two pieces before my mouth went on fire and I quickly gulped down some of my blackcurrant juice. I'd never eaten chillies that hot before.

After dinner Tamara went into another room and brought out a cake in the shape of a tropical island.

We all sang "happy birthday" and Mason blew out the twelve candles dotted amongst the palm trees.

"That is the best cake I have *ever* seen!" I squealed, turning pink when everyone looked at me.

"I had it made to remind you of our holiday in Antigua," said Tamara, kissing Mason on the top of his head.

Mason smiled. "Thanks, Mum," he said. He didn't look particularly impressed to me. He was probably used to getting birthday cakes like that, but I thought it was incredible.

After a slice of cake (which was the most delicious thing I'd ever eaten) we went back to the cinema room. We sat in the middle of the front row on seats that were covered in soft, red velvet. I sank into mine and rested my head on the back. I turned to Mason.

"You are so lucky, you know," I said. "My house is the pits."

Mason frowned. He'd been to mine loads of times.

"No it's not," he said. "It's ... friendly."

I didn't think there was anything friendly about a cold, worn-out house with thin carpets and peeling wallpaper, but I didn't say anything.

We watched some cartoons, which were really good, even though they were old. My favourite was about this wolf thing called Wile E. Coyote who lived in a desert and kept trying to catch a tall, blue bird called Road Runner. At the start you think the bird is quite stupid as it just goes around pecking at grains on the floor, but it's actually really clever and outsmarts him every time. It also says "beep, beep" before shooting off in a haze of dust, which was brilliant. Mason said that these old cartoons were his dad's favourites and they used to watch them together all the time before he got so busy with work.

After the last cartoon Mason checked his watch.

"We've got fifteen minutes until you get picked up," said Mason. "Bouncy ball?"

"Bouncy ball," I agreed. As we came out of the cinema room I skidded towards the kitchen where we'd eaten the pizza. My mouth was still burning from the hot chillies.

"I'm just going to get my drink," I yelled, as Mason headed through the dining room to open the sliding doors.

My glass of blackcurrant juice was still sitting on a place mat and I picked it up and took a big gulp. The cool liquid felt good. I took the glass with me into the dining room and put it carefully on a round table next to a vase of flowers. Mason was already outside, bouncing the ball up and down.

"I think if it's warmed up a bit, it goes even higher," he said, as I came out on to the patio. He threw the ball to me and I bounced it back.

"One!" he shouted when he caught it.

He bounced it back to me.

"Two!" I said.

We got up to twenty-two and I started giggling as I fumbled and nearly dropped it.

"Twenty-three!" said Mason, catching the ball with one hand. He circled his arm and propelled the ball towards me, but instead of it bouncing on the patio first, it hurtled straight at me. I put my hand up to shield my face and the ball careered off my arm and indoors, heading for my glass of blackcurrant juice.

"Noooooooooo!" cried Mason. We both dived up the step but it was too late. The ball hit the glass and it toppled over and rolled to the edge of the table. The purple juice poured down on to the deep, white carpet. We stared at the stain. Mason's face went pale, and then he turned to me.

"What did you leave your drink there for? You're not allowed to have drinks in here!" he shouted.

"What? But it's a dining room! How can you

not have drinks in a dining room?" I said. The blackcurrant stain seemed to be growing bigger, creeping through the plush, pristine white floor.

"Shouldn't we get something to soak it up?" I asked, feeling a bit sick. Mason ran to the kitchen and came back with a yellow tea towel. He got down on his knees and began to press it on to the juice. Before long the tea towel turned purple, but the stain didn't look any better.

"Don't you think you should tell your mum?" I said. I didn't want him to, but I thought she might know the best thing to do. Mason ignored me, pressing rhythmically on the tea towel like he was trying to revive the carpet from a cardiac arrest.

The doorbell chimed. Dad was here. We looked at each other for a moment; Mason's expression was dead serious.

"Don't say a word, OK?" he muttered through gritted teeth. I nodded. That was fine with me. He straightened my glass, closed the French doors and put the bouncy ball in his pocket. We quickly changed out of our shoes and put the blue covers on. I saw a streak of purple juice on one of Mason's new trainers. He wiped it with his hand and I breathed a sigh of relief when it disappeared. We got to the front door just as his mum was opening it.

"Hi, Dad!" I said, as soon as I saw his face. I quickly took the covers off my socks and stuffed my feet into my shoes. I wanted to get out of there as fast as possible. Dad smiled, looking a bit puzzled that I seemed to be the only guest at this party *and* that I had plastic bags over my feet. I raised my eyebrows at him and I think he understood not to say anything.

"Have you both had a good time?" Dad asked. Mason and I nodded but neither of us spoke.

Mason's dad appeared with a massive slice of cake wrapped in a napkin.

"There you go, Cole," he said. "You can share that with your little sister."

"Thank you, Mr Ferguson," I said, keeping my head down.

"They've been *so* good. We haven't really heard a peep out of them, have we, Hugh?" said Mason's mum, clearly forgetting how she'd told us to be quiet earlier. She made it sound like we were five years old, not twelve.

"It's been a pleasure to have him here," said Mason's dad. "Come back any time, won't you, Cole?"

I thought about the blackcurrant stain on their precious white carpet and swallowed.

"Thank you for having me," I said. I grunted a

"bye" at Mason and then followed Dad down the driveway. He was chatty all the way home, wanting to know what we'd been up to. I told him how much Mason liked the bouncy ball and he patted me on the back.

"See, Cole? Sometimes it's the simple presents that mean the most, you know?"

I also told him about the cinema room and the cartoon with the coyote and the big bird. He laughed and said that he was so pleased that I'd had such a good time. I decided right there and then that I wouldn't mention the blackcurrant juice.

Mabel was always spilling stuff and making a mess at home, but my parents didn't mind. I had a feeling Mason's would be much more bothered. I hoped he wouldn't be getting in loads of trouble.

CHAPTER THREE

When Dad Came to School

The first thing I thought about when I woke up the next day was the stain on the white carpet in Mason's house. My parents wouldn't be able to pay for the damage if they were asked to and I had no pocket money or savings to help.

I got out of bed and shivered. It felt like the heating wasn't working again. The air in my room was crisp and cold like it is outside. I quickly pulled on a pair of socks and shoved my arms into my dressing gown. It was too small for me and the sleeves only reached just past my elbows.

When I got downstairs Mum was still home. Usually she'd be at work by now.

"Morning, darling. I'm going in a bit later today," she said. "There's cereal for breakfast. Don't take too much."

I took a bowl out of the cupboard and shook some of the brown flakes into it. Too many fell out so I spooned a few back into the bag.

Mum was watching me, wringing her hands together. My heart sank. Mason's mum and dad must have called and told her about the ruined carpet.

"Has something happened?" I said, trying to act innocent. She took a deep breath.

"It's not good news I'm afraid, Cole," she replied. "The museum is closing down. I'm going to lose my job."

"What?!" I said. "Why?" Mum's eyes were filled with tears. My brain was quickly buzzing with a million worries. If Mum didn't have a job then how would we get any money? How would we pay bills and buy food? We didn't have enough as it was!

"Our visitor numbers are too low," said Mum. "Dr Sabine and I knew it was going to happen one day, but we hoped we could keep going for a bit longer."

Dr Sabine was Mum's one and only work colleague. She wasn't the kind of doctor you'd go to see if you had a sore throat or a broken leg – she was a doctor of history.

"But what about all the events you organized?" I said. "The *Meet an Egyptian Mummy* day and *How to be a Geologist*?"

These were special days they arranged for kids during the summer holidays. Mum sighed.

"Hardly anyone turned up, Cole. It's not surprising, we had no money to advertise. How will anyone know how special the museum is if we don't have any funds to tell people about it?"

And to make it even more upsetting, Mum absolutely loved working there. She'd planned to go to university to study history, but I came along when she was just eighteen and after that she was too busy. When I was a baby she started volunteering at the local museum and she did so well that the council gave her a part-time job. Not long after Mabel was born they offered her a full-time job, and that's when Dad started staying home to look after us.

"What will we do, Mum?" I said. "What will we do if you don't have a job?"

"Don't worry," she said, trying to smile. "I'll find something else. And your dad is still looking for work to fit in the evenings." She gave my arm a squeeze, but

I could tell she was trying not to cry.

Mabel appeared in a pair of mismatched pyjamas. She must have sensed that something was going on and she gave Mum's legs a hug.

"I just wish we could have got more people to come and visit us. It's such a shame. We've got all those treasures on display and no one is interested."

Dad came in and switched the kettle on.

"Morning, Cole," he said. "Has Mum told you the news?"

I nodded and pushed the cereal around my bowl. I wasn't hungry now.

"Don't worry," he said, patting me on the shoulder. "We'll work something out."

I watched as he gave the boiler a thump.

"There's no hot water again, Jenny," he said to Mum. "Honestly, this boiler will be the death of me." The square metal box that hung on the wall beside our back door gave a shudder, as if it was tempted to actually do something, and then it gasped and went silent. It was always breaking down.

I watched as Dad banged it again. He was wearing jeans and one of his old rock-band T-shirts. For a second, I wanted to scream at him:

"Why can't you just make this all better, Dad? Why

can't you just get a job like all the other dads?"

I thought of meeting Mason's dad last night, with his smart shirt and wide, bright smile. *He* would have plenty of money to pay for someone to fix the boiler. *He* had a proper job. Just like everyone else's fathers. What made it worse was that all my friends knew that my dad did nothing...

When Mabel was just a few months old, our teacher in primary school sent letters home asking for parents to come in for a World of Work session. Before I was born, Dad used to work as a roadie with a rock band. He got to travel all over Europe, helping to carry the band's instruments and equipment in and out of the venues and set it all up. It sounded like an amazing job and I was so pleased when Dad said he'd come and join in the session.

When we got to school my teacher, Mrs Williams, was at the door, welcoming everyone.

"Parents, thank you so much for coming! If you can make your way to the hall, I'll bring the children in after registration."

Dad gave me a pat on my head and followed the other adults. There were five of them: three dads and two mums. The other two dads were wearing suits and one of the women was wearing a green uniform.

I thought she might have been a paramedic.

After we had all said, "Good morning, Mrs Williams," we headed to the hall. My dad was sitting at the front with the other adults and Leyton's dad was setting up a PowerPoint presentation next to a big projector. Dad didn't have a presentation, he was just going to talk, but his job was going to be *far* more interesting than the others.

"Dad! DAD!" called Leyton, waving madly even though he'd only seen him ten minutes ago. I sat in the second row and beamed at my dad, who gave me a wink.

"Right, everybody, this is exciting, isn't it?" said Mrs Williams, standing at the front. "Today we have some very special guests who are kindly going to tell us a little bit about their jobs. Now, I want you to listen carefully to what the grown-up is saying, and then we can take a few questions. Shall we start with you, Mr Morgan?"

Leyton's dad clicked the laptop and grinned at us. On the projector behind him was an advert for a local estate agent.

"Hands up if your parents own their house?" said Mr Morgan. A sea of hands shot up. I kept mine down. We were living in my great aunt's house, and although we paid her to live there, we didn't own it. She gave us a discount as we were family, but on the understanding that we had to pay for any repairs.

"OK! So that's most of you," he said, pacing back and forth. "That's great! So, your parents would have come to someone like *me* to buy their house! I'm an estate agent."

Mr Morgan's presentation consisted of slides of different houses that he had sold in the local area, including how much they cost. It was quite interesting to start with as we got to see the insides of some cool places, but after a while we all began to fidget on the hard chairs. The only person not moving around was Leyton, who scowled at anyone who wasn't paying attention.

Mrs Williams asked if any of us had any questions. Someone asked about the most expensive house that he had sold and someone else asked what his favourite colour was, so Mrs Williams said it was probably time we moved on to the next guest. Kathryn Shelton's dad went next. He was a lawyer and everyone got excited as we all thought he worked with criminals and murderers, but it turned out he mostly helped people get divorced. Then it was Pia Bowman's mum, who was an optician. She showed us some of the instruments she used to do an eye examination, and Dean went to the front and tried on the big frames that they used to check what strength glasses you needed. The mum in the green uniform was after that. I was right, she was a paramedic, and she told us about how she tried to save someone's leg after they'd been a car accident. She was just getting to a really gory bit when Mrs Williams went a bit pale and stopped her, saying that we were running out of time and had to move on to the final guest.

My stomach turned over as Dad stood up and walked to the front of the class. Mrs Williams introduced him as Mr Miller and he began.

"We've heard about some really interesting jobs here this morning, haven't we?" he said. It was weird hearing my dad talking like a teacher. The class nodded and all said "yes" back to him. I couldn't wait for everyone to hear about his amazing job and all the famous bands that he'd met.

"Well, I think I might have the most important job that has ever existed. Would any of you like to guess what that might be?"

A few hands went up and Dad picked them out.

"A policeman?" said one. Dad shook his head.

"A politician?"

"A footballer?"

Dad smiled and said no to each one. I felt a bit uneasy. OK, so being a music roadie was cool, but it wasn't exactly the most *important* job in the world, not compared to being the prime minister or something.

"There are some really good answers there, but no. My job is even more important than all of those. I am a father!"

My stomach plummeted and hit the cold, wooden floor of the hall. This was a disaster. I slowly sank down in my seat and folded my arms.

"That's not a job!" shouted Trevor O'Riordan from the back.

"Oh, but it is!" said Dad. "Cole's mum works full-time and she is the person in our house who earns the money, but I still have a great deal of responsibility as my role is to look after my son and baby daughter."

I could feel my face burning. What about touring the world? The big concerts? The famous rock stars? A few people turned around and looked at me but I kept my eyes on the floor, willing him to stop speaking. Why couldn't he be an estate agent like Leyton's dad? Or a paramedic, being brave and saving lives?

Dad carried on talking about how looking after your children was a very important job, but by that point everyone had completely lost interest. Mrs Williams jumped up out of her seat and asked if anyone had any questions. I held my breath and prayed that no one would, but then a girl at the front put her hand up.

"Have you *ever* worked?"

"I have," said Dad. At last! *Now* it would get interesting. I sat upright and smiled at Dad. *Now* they'd hear all about his proper job.

"I worked in the music business and I used to tour the world alongside lots of bands."

This was more like it! I looked around and saw a flicker of interest on a few people's faces.

"But then we realized that my low pay and being away from home so much wasn't really working. I took the decision to become a full-time dad. After all, money isn't everything!"

He laughed after he said that, but the hall was silent. I hunched my shoulders and stared down at my lap. Surely the time was up now? Niall raised his hand and I groaned.

"Are you poor?" he asked, and I could see him smirking. Mrs Williams went to say something but

Dad was already answering.

"I guess if you are asking if we are poor by the amount of money we have, then yes. We are poor..."

There was a low-level gasp across the hall.

"But we are rich in other ways. We get to spend a lot of time together as a family and that is priceless."

No one said anything. I felt sick. I could tell that Dad was looking at me but I avoided his eyes. Why had I thought that he was going to talk about his roadie job? Why? We gave the parents a round of applause and after they'd left we filed back to class. Someone shoved me on the shoulder.

"That was *well* funny," said Leyton. "Poor Kid Cole! If that's your dad's job, are you his boss?"

"Does he get benefits? My uncle used to get money for doing nothing. My mum said he was lazy," said Shannon.

I wanted to cry.

Everyone looked at me differently after that. From then on I became Poor Kid Cole, a nickname that had stuck with me ever since. I was the one whose dad stayed at home and didn't work.

And now it looked like Mum was out of a job too.

CHAPTER FOUR

Marika Visits School

After Mum's bombshell about losing her job I headed off to school. I left my parents in the kitchen, talking about what they were going to do next. It didn't sound like they had much of a plan. Also, I could tell by their voices that they were worrying, and that made me feel even more panicky.

When I got to the playground everyone was buzzing about their trip to Thrill Kingdom. There was no sign of Mason so I stood behind Niall, Leyton and Dean.

"Hey, Poor King Cole!" said Niall, turning around and slinging his arm across my shoulders. "You missed such a brilliant day!"

"Yeah, the park was empty, there were no queues at all!" said Dean. "We went straight on *everything*."

"Great," I muttered, looking out for Mason. The three of them carried on chatting about all the funny things that had happened, and then there was a loud clatter behind us. We turned around. It was Isla Roberts dropping her cello case.

We watched as she adjusted a bag on each shoulder and then scooped up the large black case and struggled across the tarmac with it. Isla was some kind of musical genius. She had time off normal lessons so that she could do extra practice for national competitions, she was that good.

"There goes Mozart," said Leyton, laughing. "What a loser." Leyton seemed to find nicknames hilarious.

The bell rang and as we trooped inside I noticed one of the posters that Mason and I had put on the door was hanging on by a single pin. Today was the day Marika Loft, the famous artist, was coming to visit us.

Mason came running into our form room just before the end of registration.

"All right?" he panted, his face red. His parents left for work before he woke, so every morning he had to get himself up, have breakfast and set the house security system before going to school. He had a lot of late marks.

"All right?" I said. My stomach churned when I thought about the bright purple stain on the carpet in his house. After hearing Mum's news about her job, paying a carpet-cleaning bill was going to be impossible.

"Mason?" I said nervously. "Did your parents find out what happened?"

Mason nodded. "Don't worry about it, it's fine. I told them it was me who spilt the drink."

Relief washed through my body. I was about to thank him when our form tutor, Miss Canning, ran into the classroom.

"7A, I'm afraid there has been a change of plan for today's visit. Marika Loft isn't able to stay for the whole day after all, so you must go to your normal lessons as usual."

There was a groan from the class.

"All that clearing up we had to do and she's only going to be here for five minutes!" said Mason quietly.

"Marika's personal assistant has stated that she doesn't 'do' assemblies or go on tours of school corridors," said Miss Canning, rolling her eyes. "But she will spend some time with an art class. And I believe, 7A, that your form is due to have art this morning. Am I right?"

A few people mumbled yes and then she took the register and went through the rules about us all being on our best behaviour.

When we got to the art room, Mrs Frampton was busy rearranging easels and piles of drawing paper.

"Sit down, 7A," she cried. "Quickly now! She's going to be here *any* minute."

I sat between Mason and Isla and we watched as Mrs Frampton paced around, not really knowing what to do with herself. She got to the front of the class and stopped, placing her hand on her heart.

"Children, you've been given an incredible opportunity here. This is a once-in-a-lifetime experience and I want you to … embrace it. Today will stay with you for the rest of your lives."

"Crikey, talk about a build-up," whispered Mason under his breath.

In front of us we each had a small, square canvas and a little wooden box filled with tubes of paints, three brushes, a pencil, a small plastic dish and a bottle of water.

"Ms Loft has very kindly donated some art

materials to the school," said Mrs Frampton. "Be very careful with them. We want Marika to see what well-behaved students you are and how carefully the school would make use of any ... *financial investment* she might be willing to make to the art department." She turned and straightened one of her own paintings which had appeared on the wall behind her desk.

Isla, who was sitting the other side of me, leant forward and peered into her box. She took out a small tube of black paint, which was branded with the famous Loft logo.

"Blimey, this stuff must be well expensive," said Mason, picking out a brush which also had the Loft logo along the edge. Not only did Marika have a range of art material but she also had her own perfume, aftershave and handbags, apparently.

"Miss!" said Reilly Campbell. "Do you think she'd donate something better if we asked nicely?"

"Yeah," chimed in Pia Bowman. "Art's well boring."

"I'd rather have one of her Porsches!" yelled Spencer Walker. Everyone started chattering amongst themselves and then the classroom was filled with the clatter of the boxes being tipped out on to the desks.

"Keep your paints in your box!" shouted Mrs Frampton above the rabble.

A few brushes went flying across the room and Mrs Frampton darted around, rescuing them from the floor.

"Stop throwing the equipment around, 7A!" she screeched, crawling under a desk. "Whatever has got into you? Marika will be here any second and she won't like *any* of this—"

BANG.

The door to the classroom swung open and, just like that, Marika Loft was standing in the doorway. Her eyes quickly scanned the class. Mr Taylor, the head, was hovering behind her, his face flushed.

Mrs Frampton slowly emerged from beneath a desk at the front of the class with a bunch of brushes in her hand.

"It's you..." she said, as she stared at the famous artist.

Marika walked into the room. She was very tall and she was wearing grey, wide-legged trousers that completely covered her feet so it looked like she was gliding. Her hands were in her pockets and she was wearing a white shirt with long, puffy sleeves. Her eyes were an unnatural shade of violet and her short hair was dyed a silvery-grey and shaved on one side. As she brushed past our desk I saw a skull-and-crossbones stud in her ear. It was encrusted with diamonds that glinted against her dark-brown skin.

Everyone fell silent as the artist stood at the front of the class. We'd all forgotten the rule about not staring. She slowly looked around the hushed room and then nodded towards Mr Taylor, who was still in the doorway, clearly unsure if he should come in or not.

"I'll, erm... Shall I leave you to it then, Ms Loft? Erm ... yes. Yes, I shall," he said, practically bowing as he reversed into the corridor.

Marika's lips curled into a small smile.

"Ms Loft," said Mrs Frampton, her eyes staring down at the ground. "Can I just say what an absolute pleasure it is to—"

"Thank you, teacher," interrupted Marika, so quietly it was barely audible. "I'll take it from here. Why don't you go and make yourself a nice ... cup of tea?"

Mrs Frampton's face dropped.

"Oh ... I ... I'd quite like to stay and see how you work if that's all ri—?"

Marika closed her eyes and shook her head.

43

"I see," said Mrs Frampton. She looked at us then pressed her fingers to her lips like she was trying not to let out a sob.

A young man came into the classroom. He was wearing a grey suit and carrying a black briefcase with the Loft logo on the side. He took a bottle of water out of the case and placed it on the desk next to Marika. He whispered something in Mrs Frampton's ear, before putting his hand on her arm and guiding her towards the door.

"That must be her personal assistant," whispered Isla.

"Be good, 7A!" squeaked Mrs Frampton, as she was ushered out of the room. "Don't let me down!"

At the front of the class, Marika stood with her hands on her hips. She stared at us for so long there were a few nervous coughs. I was starting to wonder if we were supposed to do something when she finally began to speak.

"ART," she said loudly. "What … does … ART … actually … *mean*?"

We all straightened up to listen to what she was going to say next, but she was silent. Isla looked at me, her forehead wrinkled. If a teacher asked a question then Isla was always the first person to put her hand up, but she clearly wasn't sure if Marika really wanted a response.

The artist began to walk between the desks, her lilac eyes studying each of us in turn. We took sideways glances at each other, waiting to see what was going to happen next, when she suddenly stopped in front of Dean Grant. She rested her hands on his desk and leant towards him.

"You," she said, a tiny smile on her lips. "What *does* art actually mean?"

Dean turned a bright shade of pink and squirmed in his seat.

"Erm. It, erm, it means, erm ... paintings and stuff?" he said. Someone behind me snorted. Marika blinked at Dean a few times and then straightened up. She slowly walked to the front of the class and turned on a heel as she opened her arms wide. And then she spoke.

"7A," she said quietly. "It's time to make some *paintings and stuff*!"

She stood there, motionless, her arms outstretched as she stared at every single person in the class. Nobody moved. We just sat and stared back. Eventually, Kiki Gibbs raised her hand.

"Um, are we supposed to just ... start?" she said.

Marika nodded.

"You've got everything you need in your box: find a space, sit with your canvas, look around you and . . . paint."

"That's it?" said Reilly Holder. "Just paint?"

Marika smiled at her, closed her eyes and nodded again. Archie Bryce put his hand up next.

"But . . . what do we paint?" he asked. We all waited for an answer. We weren't used to being asked to do something without more instructions than this.

"Paint whatever you want. This. . ." she said, waving her hand around, "is your 'stuff'. Art is art. Anyone can make it!"

Her lilac eyes glowed as she surveyed the room. It was as if she was looking at the most beautiful scene in the world, rather than just our boring art block. She put her hands into her trouser pockets and circled us, like a shark.

"Get up from your desks and move around. Find something that really *speaks* to you. You can paint the sounds of a chair scraping on the floor or the smell of the coffee coming from the staff room or the feeling of your hand on your smooth desk. . ."

"The smell of coffee? How are we supposed to paint that?!" scoffed Hannah Clark, pulling a face.

"She's *well* weird," whispered Archie from behind me.

"I want you to express *yourselves*. I want to see *you* on the canvas."

"What, like a self-portrait?" asked Arek Nowak. Marika frowned and slowly shook her head. We were beginning to frustrate her now.

"No, not a self-portrait. But I want to feel *you* through the canvas," she said.

Arek blinked back at her. He opened his mouth to say something else but then decided against it.

"You have one hour, 7A," said Marika, glancing at her silver watch. "Three, two, one ... GO!"

We all looked at each other. A couple of girls at the front slowly picked up their canvas and paints and stood up.

"Did you see her eyes?" said Mason. "No one has lilac eyes. She must be wearing contact lenses."

Isla collected her things and moved over to some shelves. She sat on the floor cross-legged, put her canvas on her lap and began to sketch the pots of brushes.

"That's wonderful!" said Marika, spotting her. "You might choose to change your perspective to get the picture you want. Sit on the floor, stand on your chair, climb on your desk!"

Archie immediately stood on his chair and Hannah got up on to a desk and sat right in the middle. There was a moment of chaos as everyone started laughing and climbing over the furniture, but Marika just stood there, smiling.

"I'm going to paint the cars outside," said Mason. "A few blobs of paint and some wheels and I'll be done." He headed towards Mrs Frampton's desk, which had the best view of the car park. I walked around the room, trying to find a space where I could paint something, but all the best places were taken. I went to the back of the class and sat on the floor, leaning up against the wall. The sun was beating against the window and I turned my head to stare outside. The sky was the colour of a Caribbean sea and there were two aeroplane vapour trails that criss-crossed each other like a giant kiss.

From my box, I took out a little plastic dish which must be for mixing the paints. I squeezed out a few centimetres of bright blue paint and a bit of white, and I used my brush to swirl them together. It was quite thick so I added a splash of water from the bottle. The blue lightened, just like the colour of the sky, then I pressed my brush against the canvas and began to paint.

CHAPTER FIVE

Handprints

I was aware of the distant chatter of my classmates and the sound of Marika's heels tapping on the wooden floor as she walked around the room, but for most of the lesson I was utterly absorbed in what I was doing. The white vapour trails in the sky faded quickly so I had to try and remember what they looked like as I dabbed my brush on to the canvas. It was now entirely blue apart from the two wispy white lines cutting across the middle.

"Is that it?" said Niall, looking over at my picture. "That's so *boring*."

"You can't just paint the sky," said Kiki. "You've got to put *something* in it!"

I could see Marika walking around the class, nodding and smiling at everyone else's work. This was a disaster.

I picked up my picture and held it out at arm's-length to get a better look. This was the first proper painting I'd done in high school. We'd spent most of the term making a woodland collage using scraps cut out from magazines. I decided to quickly paint a tree on one side, but when I put it back on the floor, I realized that I'd accidentally made handprints in the wet paint on either side of the canvas. You could clearly see my thumbs and the outline of my hands.

I'd ruined it.

I grabbed my brush and dipped it into the blue paint, and was just about to paint over the handprints when someone shouted:

"Stop!"

I froze, my brush poised in the air. I looked up as everyone turned around to see what was going on. Marika stood in front of the window, staring directly at me, the sunlight behind her making a yellow, heavenly glow around her head.

"Don't touch it," she said, her eyes wide and bright. She lowered her voice. "H-have ... have you ... painted before?"

I shook my head. A great blob of paint fell off my brush and on to the canvas. I went to rub it in but she waved her hand at me.

"Leave it. Leave it just as it is. Put your brush down."

I looked around the class. Everyone was watching.

"What's your name?" asked Marika.

"Cole," I said.

"Cole?" she repeated, crouching down to study the picture more closely. Her wide-legged trousers brushed against the side of my picture, leaving a streak of blue paint near the hem. Those trousers probably cost more money than my mum earnt in a month.

"Yes. Erm ... Cole Miller," I said, gulping.

"I can see it. I can see *exactly* what it is you were trying to do," she said.

"You can?" I croaked. I looked down at the canvas again. The canvas covered in bright blue paint with two handprints on either side – a totally wasted hour. I braced myself for a telling-off and for everyone to start jeering.

Marika nodded.

"This is *you*, isn't it? The blue is you. You're holding your life ... your *world* in your hands."

I looked back at the painting. She must have been talking about my fingerprints on the sides.

"Oh, that's just where I picked it up and accidentally g—"

"It's … it's …" interrupted Marika, placing her hand on her heart. "It's incredible. It's telling me a story."

"It is…?" I said. She nodded. I could see Niall's face behind her, his chin practically dangling down to his chest.

"It's a picture that really *speaks* to me. It makes me want to ask *questions*."

"Right." I swallowed.

Just then, Marika's PA walked into the classroom. Marika stood up and clicked her fingers, and he hurried over.

"Declan. Get this painting into the car. We're taking it back to the gallery."

Declan looked at the canvas.

"We are?" he said, frowning.

"You are?" I said. Marika looked at me.

"Yes. But first, you need to sign it." She pointed to the left-hand corner of the canvas.

"What do I put?" I said. I'd never signed anything in my life. Marika smiled at me.

"Just put what comes naturally," she said.

I stared at the painting, dipped my brush into a darker shade of blue and did a curly *C* in the corner.

"That's perfect," Marika said, still smiling. "Would you like to give it a title as well?"

I swallowed and stared at the picture.

"Um. 'A Sky in Blue'?" I said, gritting my teeth. It sounded like a dreadful title to me.

"That's perfect," said Marika again, nodding to Declan, who reached down and picked the canvas up using just the tips of his fingers. It looked like he was used to handling wet paintings.

"Be careful, Declan. That picture is very precious," said Marika before he headed towards the car park. I was stunned. *My* painting? Precious?

"Um ... what's going to happen to it?" I said.

Marika placed her hand on my shoulder and whispered into my ear.

"We'll see, shall we?" she said with a mysterious smile.

CHAPTER SIX

The Butterfly Game

When I got home from school, Dad was putting on his coat to leave.

"Could you mind Mabel for an hour, Cole? Your mum has got a meeting after work and I need to go and talk to the bank about something."

I was too afraid to ask what he needed to discuss with them. I guess with Mum losing her job it was probably going to be something about not having enough money in our account.

"Do I have to?" I said. I really didn't like having to look after Mabel. She could be quite funny at times, but she could be scary if she had one of her tantrums. When Mabel lost it, she really, really lost it. And she always wanted to play this game that she got for her third birthday over and over again. She called it the Butterfly Game. I thought it was stupid and babyish.

"I won't be long," said Dad, putting his jacket on. "And Mum will be back in an hour, but until then, don't answer the door. Don't let Mabel eat *any* biscuits and don't leave her on her own. OK, Cole?"

Mabel danced beside me on tiptoes. She knew what was coming next: an hour with me in charge meant she could get away with more than she ever could with Dad.

Dad kissed the top of Mabel's head and managed to plant one on me too as I was too slow to duck out of the way. As soon as the front door closed, Mabel grabbed my hand and pulled me towards the kitchen.

"Biscuit, Cole. Biscuit!"

"Dad just said you can't have any biscuits, Mabel. Didn't you hear him?" I said. She ignored me as she dragged a stool to the tall cupboard where all the sweet stuff was hidden out of her reach. She climbed up and managed to prise open the door with her tiny fingers. I stood beside her, ready to catch her if she fell.

"Mabel, are you listening to me? Dad said no biscuits. You'll get told off."

There was a packet of ginger nuts sitting right at the front. Mabel's face slowly spread into a smile. It was the kind of smile that the Joker did when he knew he'd lured Batman into a trap.

"Look, Cole. Ginger nutters!" she said. "They're *open*! Please?"

We both knew that she couldn't reach the pack and needed me to get them for her. I stared at her for a moment and her face began to morph into a scowl. She started to breathe fast, sniffing in and out through her nose. If I didn't let her have a biscuit soon then she was going to go into a full meltdown.

"OK," I said, grabbing the packet. "You can have one. But don't tell Dad, OK?"

Mabel nodded, her fingers scrabbling inside the plastic. She managed to get a biscuit in each hand and clambered down from the stool.

"Butterfly time, Cole! Butterfly time!"

She ran to the bottom of the stairs as I put the biscuits back. I did it as slowly as I could but it didn't take long for Mabel to reappear with soggy crumbs around her mouth.

"Come on!" she said, grabbing my hand. I wrenched it free from her sticky grip.

"Aren't you bored of that game by now?" I asked.

Mabel's face dropped and she looked up at me through her dark lashes.

"Not bored," she said. She stuck out her bottom lip and screwed up her eyes.

"Just one game then, OK?" I said. "And I really mean it this time."

Mabel grinned, then turned and charged to the hallway and up the stairs.

When I got to Mabel's room she was already tipping the battered cardboard box upside down on to the floor. When she'd opened it on her birthday I knew straight away that it had come from a charity shop. The box was bashed up and there was a rip on the top where someone had picked off a sticker. Mabel didn't care. We were both used to second-hand things.

I sat cross-legged on her thin carpet.

"Cole help Mabel?" my sister said. I huffed and fixed the nets together while she fiddled with the little blue elephant. It had a long plastic trunk, and inside its body was a fan. You pressed the top of the elephant's head and the fan began to whir and lots of fabric butterflies shot out of its trunk and up into the air. The idea was to catch as many of the butterflies as you could in the nets. Like I said, it was a stupid game.

Mabel bashed the elephant on the head to turn it on. Every time a butterfly appeared from its trunk she'd say, "Another one!" as if she was seeing it for the very first time, rather than the millionth. She jumped around and tried to catch as many as she could in her little net. I stayed where I was and caught any that floated near me. I had to be careful not to win. If I did then that would also mean a meltdown. Eventually, butterflies stopped appearing from the trunk, so Mabel whacked it on the head to turn it off and the fan stopped whirring. She peered into my net, then into hers.

"Mabel won!" she shouted, giving me a huge grin.

"Yay," I said weakly. "How about we watch TV now?"

She shook her head and her blonde hair fell in front of her eyes.

"No," she said firmly. "More butterflies."

An hour and seventeen games later, I heard the front door open.

"Mum's home, Mabel! Come on, let's go and see her!"

Mabel stared at me for a second, then threw her net on to the floor and trotted out of her room. Freedom at last. I put everything back into the battered box and followed my sister downstairs.

"Hi, Mum," I said. Mum smiled as she pulled her shoes off.

"Hello, you two. Having fun?" Mabel did a little dance and then skipped off to the kitchen.

"How's everything? Have they changed their mind about the museum closing down?" I asked. The weird art class with Marika Loft had taken my mind off Mum losing her job for a while, but seeing her now brought it all flooding back. My stomach began to tighten.

"I'm afraid not," she said, sitting on the bottom of the stairs. "We're looking into finding new homes for all the exhibits now. It's so sad."

She rubbed at the sole of her foot. She looked very tired.

"Are you *sure* there isn't something you can do to keep it open?" I said.

"Yes, Cole. The decision has been made. Although Dr Sabine suggested a lifeline: she said that all we need to do now is to decipher 'An Enigma in Oil'. That'll solve all our problems!" She gave a half-hearted smile and took a long breath.

"'An Enigma in Oil'?" I said. "What's that?"

"It's an old painting that was given to the museum back in the early 1900s by an artist called

Basil Warrington-Jones, who was one of the main benefactors back then. There was a great deal of excitement at the time because it came with a message: whoever solves four hidden clues in the painting will find an incredible treasure. Everybody went crazy, trying to work out where the treasure was hidden, but no one ever managed it."

"When was the last time someone tried?" I asked. Mum frowned.

"Ohhh, it must have been decades ago. The 1960s, I think. The trouble is that no one really knew where to look for the treasure: there wasn't a first clue to start people off on the trail. It could be anywhere! I reckon it was just an elaborate hoax thought up by the artist to drum up publicity for his painting."

Mum sighed and got up.

"I'm going to start dinner," she said, squeezing my arm. "Try not to worry, Cole."

Mum and Dad stayed up late that night. I could hear their voices murmuring beneath my bedroom floor. I couldn't make out what they were saying, so I slowly made my way out on to the landing.

"The bank said they can't help," said Dad. "I've been to the job centre but there's nothing."

"What will we do, Doug?" said Mum, her throat

catching. "I can't face another winter in this house without any heating. It's not fair on the children."

When our boiler did decide to work, the radiators only ever got lukewarm. Last winter an engineer had said that the whole heating system ideally needed replacing, which would cost thousands.

I could hear the sound of Mum beginning to cry and Dad's soothing hushes. I didn't want to hear any more so I crept back into my room.

I got into bed and shifted lower down my mattress to where the bedsprings didn't dig in quite so much. I closed my eyes and thought about the old painting in the museum. The one that led to treasure. I felt a small fizzle of excitement deep down inside my churned-up stomach.

Maybe the time had come for someone new to try and solve "An Enigma in Oil"? And maybe that someone was me?

CHAPTER SEVEN

Getting Mason On Board

The next morning, I woke up to Dad thumping on the boiler again. I texted Mason to knock for me on his way to school, and then I had a really quick, cold shower. It's surprising how quickly you can wash when the water is so freezing it hurts.

Mum had left for work already and Dad said she would be really busy for the next few weeks, trying to find new homes for all of the exhibits.

At ten past eight the doorbell rang and I shouted bye and ran out the door. Mason was late, so we'd have to walk quickly.

"Sorry. I overslept," he said, as we headed down the road. "Dad didn't get back from Tokyo until midnight and I stayed up to see him. He was tired though, so he wasn't very chatty."

I took a sideways look at him but he was just staring down at the pavement.

"He got me this. Look!" He pushed up the sleeve of his coat to reveal a jet-black glossy watch. He tapped the face and it flashed neon-blue.

"Cool," I said. "Haven't you already got a watch?"

"Yeah... But this one's a newer model," he said, pulling his sleeve back down. I glanced at my own wrists. I wasn't wearing a coat and my school jumper was frayed at the cuffs. I quickly rolled the sleeves up to hide them, even though it was cold. Mason watched me.

"I've got a couple of jumpers I've grown out of if you want them?" he said. "I can check if Mum has thrown them out or not."

"Nah. Don't worry about it," I said.

"It's no big deal," said Mason. "I can bring them in tomorrow."

I could feel my face beginning to burn.

"It's fine," I said sharply, looking away. Mason didn't say anything else and we walked in silence for a while. We turned down the road where our school was.

"Hey, Mason," I said. "When was the last time you went to the museum?"

"Where your mum works?" said Mason. *Not for much longer,* I thought. "Not since the time we went in primary school. About six years ago? Why?"

"It's closing down. Mum is going to lose her job."

Mason frowned. "Oh no. That's too bad. Sorry, Cole."

I shrugged. "I know. But I've got an idea. Do you remember seeing an old painting in there? One with things to solve hidden in it?"

Mason thought about it for a bit.

"Nah, I just remember the mummies and the gift shop," he said. "I bought a flashing yo-yo."

"Well, my mum told me about the painting yesterday. It's like a treasure hunt and there's a prize at the end."

Mason frowned.

"And no one's solved it?" he said.

"No. Lots of people tried years ago," I said. "But now everyone has just forgotten about it."

Mason laughed. "There's probably a reason for that. Like maybe it's impossible?"

"Or maybe it isn't?" I said, smiling.

Mason sniffed. "What's this painting called, anyway?"

"'An Enigma in Oil'," I said. "And *I'm* going to solve it."

"Ha! Of course you are," he scoffed, but he stopped laughing when he saw my face. "Seriously?" he asked as we walked through the school gates and into the playground.

I nodded. "Why not? And *you're* going to help me."

"Am I?" he said. "What makes you think we can solve it?"

There was a thump from behind us.

"Ooopf. Watch it, Mozart!" shouted Niall.

"Sorry!"

It was Isla. It looked like she'd accidentally crashed into Niall. She had her school bag over one shoulder, her PE kitbag on the other and her cello case in her arms. As she walked towards us, the cello slipped and she had to duck down to stop it falling to the floor.

"The handle's broken on the case," she said. "Sometimes I wish I played a piccolo rather than this huge thing!" She started to laugh, but it came out like a snort. Mason stared at her and I smiled. She wasn't someone that we hung around with, and she quickly put her head down and rushed off.

Mason turned back to me. "She's so strange. Anyway, about that painting..."

"Someone's got to solve it, so why not us?" I said. "I need to find that treasure, Mason. I need to help Mum and Dad."

CHAPTER EIGHT

Going to the Museum

As we walked towards the museum after school, I realized for the first time just how grand it was. The old Victorian building was made of rust-red bricks with tall, white-framed windows, and beneath each window frame were draping garlands of flowers carved into the brickwork. I'd never noticed them before. On either side of the entrance were two orb-shaped lamp posts, welcoming visitors in on dark days.

"Look," said Mason, pointing to a poster by the entrance.

We walked up the steps and into the foyer. There was a welcome desk on one side, but nobody was behind it so we headed through the two carved wooden doors that led into the main hall of the museum. Mason gasped.

"Oh, wow," he said.

The room was filled with glass cases containing every stuffed wild animal you could possibly think of: lions, crocodiles, otters, badgers, buffalo, foxes, rabbits. There was even a giraffe in a really tall case that stretched up to the roof. I remembered Mum saying that stuffing animals, or taxidermy, was really fashionable in Victorian times and people didn't seem to think it was cruel back then. She said that there had been a debate about whether the displays should be destroyed, but it was decided that they should be kept for historic and scientific interest. Some of the stuffed animals were now extinct.

I remembered the smell from when I'd last visited. It was a musty and dusty smell – the kind that made your nose tickle.

"I remember this!" said Mason, stopping by an overstuffed rhinoceros. "Some thieves broke in years ago and sawed her horn off. They got in through a skylight. It was in the papers."

The story of the stolen rhino horn rang a bell. I read her sign. Apparently, a rhino's horn can be really valuable, and the thieves knew exactly what they were doing. In the article it said that her name was Rosie and that the people working in the museum at the time had replaced her stolen horn with a plastic one.

The museum was incredible. Why I had I left it so long to go back? And now it was all too late. The collection was going to be split up and sold, and the beautiful old building would probably end up being turned into posh apartments.

"I can't see this famous painting anywhere," said Mason, looking around.

"Come on, let's go upstairs and see if we can find my mum or Dr Sabine," I said. "But don't say anything about us trying to solve 'An Enigma in Oil'. I want it to be a surprise."

The upstairs gallery was full of stuffed birds, thousands of them in glass cases. We stood in front of a large cabinet containing seabirds all perched on a rock that made it look like they were just gazing out on to the ocean. There was a tiny, meshed speaker by the floor which played the sounds of crashing waves and the cries of seagulls. I stared at a large gull with yellow eyes and a fierce-looking beak.

"Ah, Cole!" said a voice. "How very lovely to see you."

Dr Sabine was walking towards us, carrying a large cardboard box. I hadn't seen her for years. I waited for her to say something about how much I'd grown but she just smiled. I liked Dr Sabine.

"Your mum is in the office. Do you want me to get her for you?" she asked, putting the box on to a table.

I shook my head.

"No, it's OK. Mason and I thought we'd come and have a look round," I said. "Mum told me you're closing down. I'm sorry."

"I'm sorry too," said Mason.

Dr Sabine sighed. "Thank you. We tried our best, we really did. It just seems that people aren't interested in museums any more. Well, not in this town, anyway."

Mason and I fidgeted a little. *We* were those people.

Dr Sabine opened the flap of the box. It was full of old books.

"Are they from the museum?" I asked.

"No, these are my reference books," said Dr Sabine. "I can't leave them behind – it would be like abandoning friends." She picked one up and gently wiped the cover with her hand.

"Did you know that this museum was famous?" she asked. "We made the front page of all the national papers once." She put the book back and rummaged in the bottom of the box, taking out an old newspaper. It was yellowed with age and looked quite fragile. On the front was a drawing of the outside of the museum with the headline:

MUSEUM'S MYSTERIOUS PAINTING WAITING TO BE SOLVED

I heard Mason gasp.

"Is that the painting that contains some kind of riddle?" I asked. "Mum told me a bit about it."

Dr Sabine smiled. "Yes, that's right: 'An Enigma in Oil'. The museum curator back then was very clever about publicizing its mysterious message. It caused an incredible amount of interest and people came here from all over the country to try and solve it. I guess it was the Victorian version of going viral."

"What's an enigma?" said Mason.

"An enigma means something that is mysterious or a puzzle," she said. "Look, that's the artist right there."

Next to the article was a photograph of a man with a large moustache. Mason read a paragraph out loud.

"*Artist Basil Warrington-Jones, 54, said of 'An Enigma in Oil': 'One simply has to look for four clues in my painting that will lead them to the riches.' There is much speculation about what treasures the painting will lead to, but Warrington-Jones has confirmed that the rewards are 'substantial'.*"

Mason looked up, his eyes wide.

"And nobody managed to do it?" I asked. "No one solved the painting and found the treasure?"

"No," said Dr Sabine, folding up the newspaper and placing it on top of the books. "There was a great deal of fuss for a few months and lots of people tried. But over time, the riddle of the painting was forgotten." She folded the lid of the cardboard box over the top of the books and unpicked the end of some brown parcel tape.

"Um, where is the painting?" said Mason.

"It's downstairs, in the foyer. You must have passed it on your way up," she said.

I nodded casually and then Mason started to do some kind of weird overacting thing.

"Oh no, is that the time?" he said as he looked at his posh watch. "We'd better get going, Cole."

He nodded his head towards the exit door. I glared at him. He was really overdoing it.

"Thank you, Dr Sabine," I said, as we edged away. We headed to the main stairs that led down to the foyer and began to walk down the carpeted steps.

"Substantial reward! Did you hear that?" I said to Mason. I *knew* this had been a good idea. A reward like that could change everything for my family!

When we got to the foyer we looked around.

"There it is!" said Mason, pointing to a wall. I stood and looked upwards. Hanging above the entrance doors was a very large oil painting in an ornately carved, rust-brown frame that must once have been shiny and golden. There was a small forest of trees on one side, and at the front was a stream, dotted with floating leaves. Standing on the right was a smart-looking man. He had a mop of brown hair and a large moustache, and he was wearing an old-fashioned suit and tie, with some strange, brightly coloured feathers pinned in a bunch on the lapel of his jacket. He stared out of the painting with dark eyes and a tight smile of amusement. I thought of my picture that Marika Loft now had back at her gallery in London. It hadn't taken me long to paint that at all. The artist must have worked on this one for months, if not years. It was huge.

"Who's he?" said Mason.

"I reckon that's Basil Warrington-Jones, the artist," I said. "He looks exactly like the man in the newspaper."

As I stared at the portrait, I imagined his lips moving:

"Think you can solve my riddle, do you, young Cole? Go on, then. Let's see what you can do..."

"I'll take some photos," said Mason, getting his phone out of his bag. He took three photographs from different angles and then I heard my phone ping as he sent them to me.

We stood and stared at the painting for a little longer and then Mason turned to me.

"Now what?" he said.

I shrugged.

"We don't really know what we're meant to be looking for, do we?" said Mason. "No wonder no one has ever solved it. Where do we even start?"

I kept my eyes fixed on the man in the painting. Mason was right. What were we trying to find?

Mason sighed as he stared at the painting on his phone, expanding his fingertips as he zoomed in.

"Hang on," he said. "There's something in the grass."

He turned his phone to me. There were two brown-coloured ears poking out of the undergrowth by the base of the trees.

"What is it?" I said, trying to zoom in closer. I looked up at the painting on the wall and squinted. It was so dark and murky it was hard to see from here, but it was much clearer on the phone.

"I think it's some kind of dog, but the ears are too big," said Mason. "It looks like a wolf!"

He handed the phone to me. He was right! It looked a bit like the coyote from the cartoons he'd shown me at his party.

We grinned at each other.

"So now what?" I said.

Mason frowned. "Basil said the clues were hidden in the painting and this wolf is hiding in the grass, so this could be the first clue! Let's have a think. What do we know about wolves?"

"Um... Little Red Riding Hood?" I said. "Howling? Full moons?"

"That's a werewolf!" said Mason, laughing.

I tried to think what else I knew about wolves, but that was it.

"Hang on. This museum might have a stuffed wolf in the natural history wing," said Mason. "Could the clue in the painting be sending us to another part of the building?"

"Maybe..." I said, as his words sunk in. "We've got nothing to lose; let's check it out!"

We both spun round and headed back to the hall full of the taxidermy animals. Mason was faster than me and he ran to the far end of the room.

"Look! This could be it," he shouted. I joined him in front of a display of four wolves standing beside some artificial shrubs. Their dark, glassy eyes stared at nothing.

We looked all around the display but couldn't find anything.

"There's got to be something," I said. "Let me have

another look at the picture."

Mason passed his phone to me.

"I don't think it's a wolf," I said. "It doesn't look quite like these."

"Hello, Cole. Hi, Mason." It was Mum. She came through a door marked PRIVATE carrying a huge bundle of papers. "Dr Sabine said that you were here."

"Hi, Mum," I said.

"Is everything OK?" she said. "I haven't seen you in here for a long time."

"Mrs Miller? We're trying to find an animal like this one. Do you know where it might be?" said Mason, showing her the close-up photo.

Mum frowned as she examined it.

"Well, it's definitely not a wolf. Its ears are too big," she said. "It looks more like a jackal to me."

Mason grinned. "Excellent!" he said, looking around. "So, where's the stuffed jackal?"

Mum shifted the heavy bundle of papers to her other hip.

"There's no taxidermy of a jackal in the museum," she said. "What's all this for?"

"Oh, we're doing this school project," said Mason. "We need to find it for ... research. Is there anything else related to a jackal in here?"

She thought about it.

"Like a canopic jar, you mean?" she said. I remembered learning about canopic jars in primary school when we studied the Ancient Egyptians. We had a go at making one out of clay.

"What's a canopic jar again?" said Mason.

"During the mummification process, all the major body organs were placed in canopic jars. There were four in all, for the stomach, intestines, lungs and liver. The jar with the head of a jackal represents a god called Duamutef. The stomach was placed in his jar," said Mum. I grinned at her. That was a really cool thing to know.

"Urgh, that's *well* gross," said Mason.

Mum began to walk across the room towards the foyer.

"Right, I've got tons of paperwork to do. We're closing up for the day now so you two better get yourselves home."

"Are there any canopic jars in the museum?" I asked, quickly following her.

Mum pushed her way through the heavy doors and dumped the papers on to the desk.

"Yes, we have some in the Egyptian gallery," she said.

My spine tingled. This was brilliant! All we needed to do was to find the jar with the jackal's head and take a look inside.

"Come on! Let's go!" said Mason.

"Whoa, hang on a minute," said Mum. "I just told you! We're closing for the day. You'll have to come back another time."

She looked fed up with us but I knew it was just because she was under so much stress. And she didn't realize I was trying to help.

"But we'll only be five minutes. Please?" I begged. Mum went to the wall and turned the lights off and the room went dark.

"Home, Cole. No more discussion," she said. "I'll be back after I've got through this lot. I'll see you later."

She went through the door marked PRIVATE as we made our way back to the glowing green exit sign. I shivered as we walked past the dead animals in the darkness.

"Mason?" I whispered, stopping to look at a tiger with its jaws open wide. "Do you think Basil's treasure is in the museum somewhere?"

Mason shrugged. "Who knows? I don't expect he thought anyone would actually solve the riddle. Let's come back tomorrow and find the jackal jar and see if there's anything there."

I stared at the tiger's teeth and at the muscles rippling on its shoulders. It was in a crouched position, as if it was just getting ready to pounce.

"No," I said. "This can't wait any longer. I need to find that treasure fast. Let's go and look now. Be really quiet so my mum doesn't catch us."

When we got to the foyer I glanced up at the artist staring down from his own oil painting. His eyes twinkled in the gloom and I thought I saw his moustache twitch. I shuddered as we crept up the stairs to the Egyptian gallery. It felt like Basil Warrington-Jones was watching us.

CHAPTER NINE

The Canopic Jar

"Do you think this place is haunted?" whispered Mason, as we walked along the top gallery that overlooked the natural history room. I could see the dark shape of the large giraffe, its head nearly reaching us.

"Definitely," I said. "I reckon the ghost of Basil Warrington-Jones is lurking behind us right now, don't you? He's probably really angry that we're about to solve his riddle."

Mason laughed nervously. It was almost pitch black but there was a sliver of light shining from beneath a door straight ahead of us. We went through it and along another corridor, past an

Iron-Age display and through some more doors towards the back of the museum. It was so still and quiet everywhere. We turned a corner but it was a dead end, filled with a large model ship in a glass case.

"Look!" said Mason, pointing at a sign leading to the Egyptian gallery. We hurried along the corridor but abruptly stopped when we spotted a figure ahead of us.

"It's Dr Sabine," I whispered. We both watched as she turned through the doors into the Egyptian gallery.

"That's it then," said Mason. "We'll have to come back tomorrow."

Just then a mobile phone began to ring. Dr Sabine emerged back through the doors.

"Dr Sabine speaking," she said. "Yes, yes . . . hang on, I'll just move where there's a better signal." She walked further down the corridor and through a door, which clicked softly closed behind her.

"Come on!" I said, grabbing Mason's arm. We ran into the Egyptian gallery, jumping as the sounds of a busy, bustling market surrounded us. Our movements must have triggered a sound effect. We walked past a few cases filled with old tools. On top of one was a clipboard and a bunch of keys that must have belonged to Dr Sabine.

"We'd better be quick," said Mason, checking the other cabinets. "Look! Here it is!" I went and joined him. Inside the cabinet were four dusty canopic jars, one with the head of a hawk, one with a baboon's, one with the head of a man and one with a jackal's.

"That's it!" I said. "That's exactly like the one hiding in the painting!" I read the small white card that was positioned below it.

"*A jar with the jackal head of Duamutef who guarded the stomach*. How are we going to look inside it?" I said.

"Let's see if we can open the cabinet," said Mason, checking the front.

I knelt down and looked around the back. There was a small silver latch with a keyhole.

"We need a key!" I said, crawling back out. I ran over to Dr Sabine's bunch. "There's hundreds on this!" I said, fumbling through them. Mason grabbed them off me.

"It must be this one," he said. He held up a little key with a number five embossed on it and then pointed to a silver sticker with the number five in the corner of the cabinet. I hadn't even spotted that.

"What about the alarms?" I said. "They might be linked to the police station or something."

"If we set off an alarm we just take a quick look in the jar, lock the case, throw the keys back down and say that you accidentally nudged the glass or something."

I was about to object to it being *me* who would take the blame for nudging the glass when he dived on to the floor, crawled to the back of the cabinet and undid the lock. He slowly opened the side and we both stared at each other, waiting for an alarm to go off. Nothing happened.

"Get the jar!" I said. "Dr Sabine might be back any second!"

"But what if it's still got some dead guy's guts in it?" he said, kneeling by the cabinet.

"Of course it hasn't!" I said. "Oh, I'll do it."

He moved out of the way and I slowly stretched my arm towards the jar.

"Wait!" hissed Mason. I froze. "Aren't you supposed to be wearing white gloves?"

I glared at him.

"We haven't got time for that now!" I said. I leant in and grabbed the jar. I was expecting it to feel smooth but it actually felt quite rough. I held it close to my chest and slowly removed the jackal-headed lid. I was almost frightened to look in case Mason was right and it was full of ancient intestines. I held it towards the light and we both peered inside.

Empty.

I turned it upside down and a tiny roll of paper fell out on to the floor, just as I heard Dr Sabine's voice getting louder as she approached the room.

"Hurry!" said Mason. I fumbled with the lid and shoved the jar back in the cabinet. Mason closed the door, locked the silver latch and threw the keys on top of Dr Sabine's clipboard while I picked up the scroll of paper and slipped it into my pocket, and then we both jumped behind a wooden sarcophagus. We stood, still and silent, and listened as Dr Sabine picked up her keys and clipboard and walked to the corner of the room.

Mason grabbed my arm and we quietly crept to the door and out without her even knowing we were there. As soon as we reached the corridor we began to run back to the foyer and down the carpeted stairs.

It was much lighter there and I blinked as my eyes adjusted. I took the tiny scroll out of my pocket.

"What's it say?" said Mason. I carefully unrolled the piece of paper. Something was written in faint ink.

"*Look beside my feet,*" I read.

"His feet?" said Mason. We both stared up at the painting again. Basil Warrington-Jones was standing in the grass beside the river. There was nothing beside his feet, apart from a small rock.

"I don't get it," said Mason. "There's nothing there, just that rock. What's the point of that?"

I took out my phone and found the photo that Mason had taken when we'd first seen the painting. I zoomed in on the area by Basil's feet to see if there was anything that we were missing. Nothing.

"I can't believe we found the second clue but now we're stuck again," I said.

My phone pinged. It was a text from Dad telling me that dinner would be ready in twenty minutes.

"I've got to go," I sighed. "Let's decide what to do next in the morning."

"Yeah, OK," Mason said. "At least we've solved one clue though, eh? That's one more than anyone else has ever managed!"

He was right. But I had a feeling that Basil Warrington-Jones was still one step ahead of us.

CHAPTER TEN

Asking Isla for Help

When I got home, Dad was stirring a bolognese on the cooker and Mabel was sitting at our small kitchen table scribbling a crayon over some old newspaper. Our boiler rattled away on the wall. Dad gave it a thump. It stopped shaking and gave a low, growling noise.

"Oh, Mabel, not on the floor!" sighed Dad. Mabel had started rolling her crayons off the kitchen table, one by one. I bent down to help him pick them up, but as soon as we put the crayons back on to the table, my little sister was rolling them off again.

"MABEL! STOP IT!" yelled Dad. Mabel's bottom lip did a pre-meltdown wobble and then she began to cry.

"Cole, can you take her into the front room and put something on the telly while I get dinner finished?" Dad shouted above her wails. The hob began to fizzle and he leapt towards it, turning the heat down on a pan of water that was bubbling over.

"Come on, Mabel," I said, scooping her up. "Let's see what's on TV, shall we?"

Mabel stopped crying and wiped her nose on my shoulder. Great. Now I had snot on my one and only school jumper. I took her into the lounge, plonked her on to the sofa and put the TV on, choosing a cartoon about an allotment where all the vegetables could talk. Mabel stared at the screen. I heard the front door bang as Mum came in from work. I went out to the hallway. Dad had an envelope in his hand with FINAL written across the top in red. Mum took out the letter and read it. Her eyes crinkled up and Dad rubbed her arm.

"Oh, Cole!" she said, spotting me. "I didn't see you there." She quickly folded the letter and Dad took it as he went back to the kitchen.

"What was that?" I asked.

"It's just a bill, that's all," she said. "Nothing to worry about." But I could tell by their faces that it was definitely something to worry about.

Over dinner Mum and Dad were really quiet, so I tried to cheer them up by telling them what had happened with Marika Loft when she came to visit our school. I hadn't told them anything about it yet.

"We all had to do a painting each and she said my one was really good. She's taken it back to her gallery in London!" I said.

"That's nice," said Mum, but I could tell she wasn't really listening. Dad got up and thumped the boiler, which had started to shudder again.

"She's got houses all over the world and even has her own personal assistant!" I continued. "He was the one who took my painting back to the gallery."

Mum scraped her food around on her plate.

"Sorry, love, I'm not very hungry tonight," she said to Dad. "I'll start clearing up."

Dad couldn't have been hungry either as he got up to help her.

"Cole?" said my little sister, her chin all orange from the bolognese sauce. "Can Mabel see your painting?"

I guess at least someone had been listening.

"You can't, I'm afraid, Mabel," I said. "I just told you. Marika has taken it to her art gallery in London."

Mabel frowned at me.

"Why?" she said.

I twirled the spaghetti on to my fork.

"I guess she must have really liked it,' I said. "I didn't think it was very good, but she seemed really impressed. And I don't *think* she was joking. . ."

As I finished eating I watched Mum as she scraped her dinner into the bin. She looked so miserable. If only I could help by solving 'An Enigma in Oil'.

I thought about the jackal head jar and the little note.

"*Look beside my feet,*" I whispered to myself. "What does it mean?"

I didn't have a clue. Having Mason on board to solve the mystery was brilliant, but I had the feeling we might need extra help.

The next day in form, Leyton and Niall were waiting for me.

"Poor Kid Cole! Here he comes," said Leyton. "Still wearing your coat from primary school, are you?"

It was true. And it was shabby and too small. I took it off and screwed it into a ball. I hated this coat but it was the only one I had. As I stood there in my jumper I realized there was still a snot stain on my shoulder where Mabel had wiped her nose. I quickly brushed at it.

"Just think of all the coats he could buy when Marika sells his painting for millions!" said Niall. "What was it called again? 'A Sky in Blue'? More like 'A Sky of Poo'!"

"She's probably taken it back to show everyone how *not* to paint. You should see if you can get some kind of commission for that, Cole!" said Leyton.

They both collapsed into laughter as I sat down heavily. It was more important than ever that I solve the mystery of the painting and find the treasure – then Niall and Leyton would never be able to make jokes about my family being poor again. They'd have to shut up once and for all.

Mason sat down beside me. I quickly turned to him.

"You know that hundreds of people have tried to solve 'An Enigma in Oil' and failed?" I asked. He nodded.

"Well, I think we need help," I said. "We can't work it all out on our own. We need someone with a really, really massive brain."

"Yeah, you're probably right," said Mason. "But who?"

Just then, someone came crashing through the classroom door. Miss Canning looked up as Isla ricocheted off her desk with her huge cello case.

"Can't you leave your instrument in the music room today, Isla?" said our form tutor. "We're quite crowded in here as it is."

Isla dropped her eyes.

"It's being used for other things so Mr Norris said I had to keep it with me. Sorry, Miss."

"OK, not to worry," said Miss Canning. "I have a letter here for you to pass on to your parents. The head of year wanted to put in writing how pleased we are with your progress this year across all subjects. Well done, Isla."

Isla's neck turned a shade of pink which spread up to her cheeks. It was like a strawberry milkshake was slowly being poured into her head. She took the envelope from Miss Canning and stuffed it under her armpit, then made her way to her seat, whacking a few tables with the cello as she went.

Mason looked at me and wiggled his eyebrows.

"I think we've found someone to help, don't you?" he whispered. I grinned and watched as Isla sat down.

We didn't usually talk to Isla much. No one did. She was always around but you never really noticed her, unless she was crashing into you with her cello. It was well known that she was the smartest student in our year and there was a rumour that her parents were incredibly pushy. I wasn't sure if that was true or not.

We decided we'd try and talk to her at lunchtime and we found her sitting on a bench on her own around the back of the language block. The black cello case was propped up behind her.

"Yes?" she said, looking at us suspiciously as we stood by the bench. She unwrapped a cheese sandwich and began to nibble the crusts as she waited for us to say something. I sat down.

"Sorry to disturb you, Isla," I said. "It's just that we've got a puzzle that we're trying to solve and, well, we wondered if you'd like to help?"

She blinked at me.

"What puzzle?" she said. Her eyes darted to Mason and then back to me. I sat down.

"There's a painting in the town's museum that contains some kind of treasure hunt," said Mason. "It's called 'An Enigma in Oil'."

She smirked.

"Do you know it?" said Mason, sitting on her other side.

"Of course. Doesn't everybody?" she said. She took a carton of apple juice out of her bag, pierced the top with the small straw and began to sip.

"Mason and I are going to solve it," I said. We waited as she drank. The carton of juice made a spluttering sigh as she squeezed the last few drops through the straw with her fist. She gave a little gasp and dropped the squashed carton into her lunchbox.

"How on earth are you going to do that? No one has solved it for over a hundred years." She picked up her sandwich and carried on eating.

"I don't know. But we're going to try," I said.

She began to giggle.

"What's so funny?" asked Mason.

"I don't mean to be rude but I don't think you've got much chance." She finished the last mouthful of sandwich and took out a chocolate biscuit. She was being really annoying.

"We'd have more of a chance if you helped us," said Mason. "You're, like, the cleverest person we know." He grinned at her and she smiled back at him then dropped her eyes to her lap.

"How far have you got?" she said, looking up again.

Mason fidgeted in his seat. "Well, *I* spotted a jackal hidden in the grass," he said. "Cole here thought it was a wolf, but I said it was definitely a jackal."

"What?" I said, glaring at him. He grinned at me as Isla began to laugh.

"Anyway," said Mason, "that led us to a canopic jar in the Egyptian gallery."

Isla's eyes widened.

"Brilliant!" she said. "Duamutef. The god that guards the stomach."

"Yeah! That's the one," said Mason. "So, anyway, we looked in the canopic jar and we—"

"Hang on," said Isla. "Did you handle the exhibit?"

"Cole did!" said Mason quickly. Isla shot me a look.

"Well ... I did ... but that doesn't matter. What *does* matter is that we found a message," I said. "It was *inside* the jar."

Isla stared at me. "And what did it say?" she said.

"It said, *Look beside my feet*," said Mason, all dramatically.

"We went back to examine the painting, but there's nothing there. Just a rock," I said. "We wondered if you could come to the museum after school and see if you can spot anything yourself? Seeing that you've got an extra big brain and everything!"

Isla didn't laugh. She didn't seem to find me as amusing as Mason. She finished her chocolate biscuit and began to pack her rubbish away into her lunchbox.

"OK," she said. "But you'll have to wait for me until I've finished cello practice."

"Fantastic!" said Mason.

"That's brilliant. Thanks, Isla," I said.

She put the plastic box into her school bag, swung it up over her shoulder and then went around to the back of the bench to pick up her cello.

"Do you ... um ... want a hand with that?" said Mason. I noticed his face flushed a little as he spoke.

Isla stared at him, blankly.

"No, thanks," she said. The bell went for the end of lunch and as she turned away she smashed the end of the bench with the big, black case.

Did the three of us *really* have any hope of solving the enigma? I wasn't sure.

CHAPTER ELEVEN

Beneath Basil's Feet

"How long is she going to be?" asked Mason. He checked his watch for the sixth time. "Maybe we should go and see if she's still in the music room."

I was sitting on a bench, trying to mend the zipper on my coat. Not only was it too small, but now the zip had come off the runner and I couldn't get it to go back on.

"She'll be here," I said. "Just relax."

The zip moved some of the way and then it got stuck completely.

"I've got a spare coat you could have, if you like," said Mason. "I've barely worn it."

I could imagine that Mason had a selection of

coats. Probably one for every day of the week.

"It's all right. This one is fine," I said, pulling on the zipper.

"It's not though, is it?" said Mason. "It's too small, you've bust the zip and it's really thin. You must be freezing."

I glared up at him.

"I said it's fine." I pulled the coat around me, giving up trying to mend the zip.

"Here she comes!" said Mason as Isla walked out of the main doors. She looked different and it took me a few seconds to work out why – she wasn't carrying her cello. She seemed lighter, as if she had a bounce in her step.

"Hi!" she said with a shy smile. "Are we ready?"

"Thanks again for this, Isla," I said as we began to walk. "We really appreciate it."

"That's all right," she said. "It makes a change from playing the cello! What made you decide to try and solve this mystery? That painting has been in the museum for ever – why are you interested in it now?"

Mason didn't say anything. I thought about it for a second and decided to be honest.

"My mum is about to lose her job," I said. "If I can find the treasure then my family won't need to worry about money any more."

Isla didn't laugh or jeer at me, she just nodded. I guess *everyone* knew that "Poor Kid Cole" didn't have any money.

"And I said I'd help him because I've got such an exceptional brain," said Mason. Isla giggled.

"If we find the treasure we'll split it three ways, OK?" I said.

Isla shook her head.

"No way. This whole thing is your idea. It's your prize," she said.

Did she feel sorry for me too? I felt a flicker of shame but shook it off. The museum would only be open for another couple of weeks. I couldn't let anything hold me back now.

When we arrived at the museum foyer we turned around and stood staring up at the painting above the entrance.

"Gosh, it's incredible," said Isla. "Where's the jackal?"

"Just there." Mason pointed towards the tall grass.

"And the last clue said, *Look beside my feet*," said Isla to herself. She squinted towards the image of Basil Warrington-Jones and walked up and down as we watched her.

"There's some kind of rock there, by his feet, but I agree. There's nothing else."

My heart sank. I'd really hoped that she would find something. She headed to the staircase and walked halfway up, turning to face the painting.

"Now what?" said Mason.

"I don't know," I said, my stomach churning. "That's it, I guess. We've got as far as we can go already. We'll never find it." It had been stupid of me to expect we'd actually get somewhere. Good things never happened to me.

Isla came back down the stairs, looked up at the painting, then went back up again.

"What's she doing?" whispered Mason.

"I dunno," I said, watching her as she moved along one step to the far right. She suddenly turned to us, a huge grin on her face.

"Have you guys ever heard of Holbein's skull?" she said.

"A skull?" said Mason.

"Yes. There was a German artist called Hans Holbein the Younger and he painted a picture of two men standing in front of cabinet."

"Sounds thrilling," said Mason.

"The thing is, that painting had a secret. At the front are some white shapes. They don't really look like anything from face-on, but if you stand and look at the painting from a certain angle then the strange shapes reveal exactly what they are – a human skull."

"Wow!" I said.

"It's amazing," said Isla. "And I think that's exactly what Basil Warrington-Jones has done here. Come up and I'll show you."

Mason and I joined her.

"Now, look beside Basil's feet," she said. "What do you see?"

"A rock," said Mason. Isla nodded.

"Great, now take a few steps to the right and *then* look at it. What do you see now?"

Mason and I shuffled along the step and looked at the painting. The rock had changed: what had looked like shadows and curves from the front had been transformed into lines that resembled billowing sails.

"It's a ship!" I shouted.

"Exactly!" said Isla. She ran down the stairs and grabbed three leaflets from the welcome desk.

"Here," she said, running back to us. "See if there's anything to do with ships or naval history in the museum."

Mason opened his leaflet to a map in the centre while Isla studied hers.

"I can't see anything," said Mason. I didn't need to look. Mum had never mentioned anything to do with naval history before. Isla folded up her leaflet and paced back and forth.

"Maybe it's not part of an exhibition? Maybe it's just something you'd walk past and not really notice," she said.

I gasped and they both stared at me.

"Mason, do you remember when we went to the Egyptian gallery we passed a model ship?" I said.

Mason frowned. "Um. No," he said. "It was dark. And scary. I wasn't really looking."

"It's at a dead end in the corridor by the stairs. Come on!" I said.

CHAPTER TWELVE

HMS Caroline

The three of us stared at the model ship as our breath fogged against the glass case.

"That's pretty incredible," said Mason. And it was. It was formed of two different shades of wood with hundreds of tiny criss-crossed strings that made the rigging. Along the sides were rows of little guns poking out through square holes, and at the front was a heavy-looking anchor. The figurehead was of a man wearing a waistcoat and a cravat.

"It says here that this is a model of the *HMS Caroline* and it was made by French prisoners of war," said Isla, squinting at a sign in the gloomy light. "Let's see if we can find any clues."

"I'll look around the back," said Mason, edging his way along the side of the case. There wasn't much room as the case was squashed right up against the wall.

"Hold on, there are some things underneath the boat," said Mason. "There's a sword, a telescope ... and some weird thing like a ruler with a short telescope."

I made my way along the wall to join him and Isla squeezed in beside me. She got her phone out and turned on the torch, pointing it into the case.

"That's a sextant," she said. "It's an instrument that they used in olden days for celestial navigation."

Mason and I went quiet.

"Celestial what?" said Mason.

"They used them to measure the angular distance between the horizon and a planet or the moon or a star," she said. "That way you could work out where you were in the world."

"How do you know all this stuff?" I said.

Isla crouched down.

"I read a lot," she said. "Never underestimate the power of books and what you might learn from them."

She angled her torch so that it shone right on the

sextant. "And I think this might have something to do with the next clue. It's a guide for sailors and it could be guiding us towards solving 'An Enigma in Oil'. Can you see anything now there's a light on it, Mason?"

Mason was the closest and he peered in.

"No. It's just made of brass and glass and a bit of wood. Oh . . . hang on. There's a piece of paper tucked underneath it!"

"What does it say?!" I said. "Does it tell us where the treasure is?" My stomach did about eight flip-flops.

Mason crouched down and put his head on one side.

"It's the same handwriting as the note in the canopic jar!" he said. "It says, *Listen to the river.*"

"*Listen to the river*?" I said. "What on earth does that mean?"

He stood up and we came out from beside the cabinet. I paced around.

"Maybe the treasure is in a river? Is there a river in the town? Isla? I don't think we have a river anywhere near here. Do we? Do either of you have *any* ideas where it might be?" I knew I was rambling but I couldn't help myself.

Isla shook her head. "We need to take some time

and think about it," she said.

"But I don't have time!" I shouted. "My mum is going to be out of a job soon and we won't have any money to pay for food or bills or anything! We need to find that treasure!"

I looked away and felt Mason's hand on my shoulder.

"Mate. We've only just found the second clue. Just relax, OK?"

I shrugged his hand off. It was OK for him – he had *everything*.

"Mason is right," said Isla. "Let's have another look at the painting on our way out and then we can all go home and have a think."

I sighed. They were right but I just felt a sense of panic. Every day we hadn't solved the puzzle was another day closer to my family having no more money.

We made our way back to the foyer, but when I looked up at Basil's painting, the river just looked like a few ripples and floating leaves to me.

"I can't see anything, can you?" said Mason. I shook my head.

I looked at Isla. She was staring at the river and blinking a lot.

"Any ideas, Isla?" I asked.

"No. Sorry," she said. She took her phone out of her pocket, held it up and took a picture of the painting. "I'd better get going. I'll see you tomorrow." And then she quickly headed out of the large wooden doors.

When I got home from the museum I sat on the bottom of the stairs and stared at the thin, threadbare rug that stretched the length of our hallway. Mabel came and sat beside me. The house was freezing and she was wearing leggings and two jumpers but no socks. Mabel hated wearing socks. The end of her nose was a little red circle.

We were listening to Dad, who was talking on the phone in the lounge. He hadn't heard me come in.

"... and I was wondering if we went ahead with the new boiler, whether we'd be able to pay in instalments?" he said to the person on the phone. "Boilers don't come cheap, do they?" He laughed, but I could tell it was a nervous laugh and not a real one. It went quiet as the person on the other end of the phone replied.

"I understand," said Dad. "But we wouldn't be able to pay the whole balance as soon as the work had been done, you see. I can't put my family through another winter without heating. If we could just pay a little each month then. . ."

The person on the phone must have interrupted as Dad stopped talking again. Mabel looked at me. She didn't understand what was going on but she must have sensed that she should be quiet.

"I see," said Dad. "In that case, I'm afraid we won't be requiring your services. Thank you."

"Come on, Mabel," I whispered as my little sister reached up and placed her cold fingers in my hand.

CHAPTER THIRTEEN

Mr Taylor's Office

The next day in form, Miss Canning said that there was a phone call for me in the head teacher's office.

Everyone turned and stared. Nobody got phone calls in the head teacher's office. Mason gave me a nudge.

"Who is it?" he said.

"How would I know?" I said. I didn't like it. Maybe something bad had happened at home?

I stood up, scraping my chair behind me.

"I bet your dad has found a job at last," whispered Niall into my back. "That would be the top news story of the day, eh?" Leyton, who was next to him, found this utterly hilarious and whacked his hand on the desk in appreciation. Isla was sitting across the gap and she glared at them both, then gave me a small smile.

When I got to reception the secretary told me that Mr Taylor was waiting for me in his office. I knocked lightly on his door and went in. He was on the phone.

"...Yes, he has an incredible talent... Yes, yes, we have noticed it ourselves even at this early stage..."

He quickly beckoned for me to sit down.

"Ah, yes ... yes..." he continued on the phone. "Well, the star pupil is sitting here with me now, so would you like to convey the good news to him?"

Mr Taylor paused and then passed the receiver over the desk. I took it, but I didn't like not knowing who was on the other end.

"Um. Hello?" I said.

"Cole Miller?" said a woman's voice.

"Yes?" I said.

"Marika Loft here. How are you today?"

Marika Loft? The artist? I couldn't believe it.

"I'm ... um ... I'm all right, I s'pose," I said. Mr Taylor mouthed two words at me from across the desk:

"*Speak posher!*" he said. I frowned at him.

"And ... er ... how are you today, Marika Loft? I

mean Mrs, Miss, Ms Loft?" I said. Mr Taylor grinned at me and gave me a double thumbs-up.

"That's very kind of you to ask but I'm not phoning about me, Cole," said Marika. "I'm calling about you. Or, more importantly, your painting."

"My painting?" I said. She must have meant the one she'd taken back to her gallery.

Mr Taylor was staring at me so I twisted to one side. He was putting me off.

"'A Sky in Blue' has caused quite a stir, Mr Miller. My gallery has been buzzing all week," said Marika.

"A stir?" I said. "What kind of stir?"

I could sense Mr Taylor waving his arms at me but I didn't look at him.

"I have a very important client, a very . . . *generous* client who is a great supporter of my work and of the art world. He has made an offer for your painting."

"An offer?" I said. My heart began to pound.

"Yes. And I have accepted it on your behalf. I hope that is OK, Cole?"

"I'm sorry. Did you say you've accepted an offer?" I repeated. My ears were ringing.

"Yes. For one thousand pounds."

The phone line went silent.

"A THOUSAND POUNDS?!" I shouted.

Mr Taylor had moved around to the side of the desk and his face appeared in front of mine.

"*Stop repeating her! She won't like it!*" he hissed.

"Yes. One thousand," said Marika. "I'll waive my fee but I'd have to take a percentage of future sales. And he's *very* interested to know when you'll be producing more work."

I didn't know what to say apart from, "More work?", so I just kept quiet so I didn't repeat her again. This was incredible! My painting was worth that much money? It didn't seem real. Mum and Dad were not going to BELIEVE THIS!

"You have a remarkable talent, Cole. I can't wait to see what you will paint next. Declan, my PA, will be popping by your house later today to drop off some art material for you. We'll present a new painting to the public in a few weeks' time. How does that sound?"

I swallowed. I had to do another one?

"OK... I guess," I said. "And they actually liked it? The person who bought it? Are you sure they're not going to change their mind?"

I heard Marika chuckle.

"They loved it, Cole. Now, when you start your next piece, I want you to be mindful of the things that worked so well in your first. Your use of colour was wonderful. And your painting made me want to ask *questions*. OK?"

"Right," I said, thinking of the blue canvas with my handprints and two criss-crossed lines. I didn't really understand what she meant about questions but I was too embarrassed to ask.

"Let the painting *speak* to you first. Then begin," she continued.

I had literally no idea what she was talking about but I didn't care. Dad could get the boiler fixed at last! They wouldn't have to worry about us not having any heating for the winter! My face ached from how widely I was grinning.

"Now, pass the phone back to your head teacher," said Marika. "And well done again, Cole. This is a very exciting time for you. I'm sure your next painting will go for much more."

"Thank you!" I said. "Bye!" I gave the phone back to Mr Taylor in a daze.

"Ah, Ms Loft. Can I possibly have a quick chat about our plans to refurbish the art department? Would you be interested in making an ... um ... financial contribution?"

While he was talking, Mr Taylor scribbled

something on a scrap of paper and passed it across the desk:

Get to your first lesson now. I'll let you give your parents the good news tonight! Well done, Cole!

I got up and walked out of his office in a state of shock. I couldn't believe what had just happened. A thousand pounds! Just for a painting! By me! It was unreal. When I walked into my maths class everyone turned and stared at me.

"All OK, Cole?" said my teacher, Mrs Hart. I nodded and sank down beside Mason.

"OK, 7A, I've given you some long multiplication questions on your sheets. I'll give you ten minutes to work through those and we can see how much you learnt from last lesson," said Mrs Hart.

Everyone leant over their desks and began to work but I just stared straight ahead. I was too busy picturing a pile of money to concentrate. If I sold more paintings, who knew what could happen? Mum wouldn't have to worry about the museum closing down. This could change our lives! Mason was staring at me.

"What's going on?" he whispered. I looked back at

him and grinned.

"You know that painting I did? The one that Marika Loft took back to her gallery?" I whispered.

"That blue thing with your handprints on it?" He sniffed.

"Yes," I said. "You'll never guess what? It sold. For a thousand pounds."

"WHAT?!" he shouted.

"Mason Ferguson! Concentrate on your work, please," said Mrs Hart crossly, looking up from her desk. We both put our heads down and pretended to be busy with our sheets.

"A thousand pounds?" he whispered. "For *that* thing? Are you sure?"

I nodded, slightly annoyed that he thought it was so bad. Mason shook his head in amazement.

"And that's not all," I said, keeping an eye on Mrs Hart. "She wants me to do another one!"

"You're kidding," said Mason, his jaw falling open in shock. I shook my head. He looked away to check on Mrs Hart and then back at me again.

"And she thinks it'll sell?"

I nodded. "Yes. Can you believe it?!"

Mason gazed into the distance. "A thousand pounds," he said. Then he gasped. "The next one might sell for more! If the person who wants to buy it is really keen, or stupid, they might pay tens of thousands for an original 'Cole Miller' painting!"

We both snorted. This was *crazy*.

"Mate! You're gonna be rich!" Mason grinned and slapped me on the back.

I laughed as I let those amazing words sink in, but I was already feeling a bit worried. I stared down at the first question on my maths sheet and my head began to spin a little.

What on earth was I going to paint next?

CHAPTER FOURTEEN

The Announcement

I decided I'd wait until Mum got in from work before I told them my good news. I did my homework in my room and after an hour I heard the front door bang closed. I ran downstairs.

"Mum! Something BRILLIANT happened today!" I said, jumping from the third step. "It's about my painting!"

Mum took her coat off. Under her eyes there were two dark rings. She looked exhausted.

"What painting?" she said, slipping her shoes off.

I *knew* she hadn't been listening the other night.

"The one I did at school when Marika Loft came to

visit. She took it back to her gallery, remember? Come on! I've got to tell Dad too."

I grabbed Mum's arm and dragged her into the kitchen.

"Dad!" I said. "Are you listening? I've got some news!"

Mabel was grinning and clapping her hands together, realizing that something exciting was going on.

"All OK, Doug?" said Mum. "You look like I feel."

"There's no hot water, I'm afraid," said Dad. "The boiler has completely packed up now. I'll boil the kettle for a bath." He switched the kettle on and it began to rumble.

"Mum! Dad!" I said. "I'm trying to tell you something!"

Dad frowned at me as I turned the kettle off.

"I need to tell you about my painting! Something amazing has happened!"

"Cole's painting!" said Mabel, joining in.

"Sorry, love," said Mum. "What was it you wanted to tell us?"

I grinned at them both.

"Marika Loft rang the school today and I had to go to the head teacher's office and speak to her. She's sold my painting for a thousand pounds!"

Mum plopped a teabag into a mug, then looked up at me.

"Sorry? What did you say?" she said.

"Marika Loft took my painting to her gallery in London. She thought it was really good! And some man bought it for a thousand pounds!"

Mum stared at me for a moment and then shook her head and turned the kettle back on.

"Very funny, Cole," said Dad.

"But it's true!" I yelled above the noise of the kettle. "It was called 'A Sky in Blue' and Marika Loft took it to her gallery in London. It really has sold!"

I looked at Mum and then at Dad.

"And that's not everything!" I said. "Marika wants me to paint another one! She said that it might make even *more* money!"

The doorbell rang. Mum huffed and turned towards the hallway.

"I'm not in the mood for jokes, Cole," she said. "They gave us a closing date for the museum today. In three weeks' time I'll be out of a job."

The bell rang again and I followed Mum as she opened the door. It was Declan, Marika's assistant.

"Ah, Mrs Miller, a pleasure to meet you. I've brought the materials for Cole," he said, nodding towards a large box in his arms. He spotted me over Mum's shoulder. "Hi, Cole, huge congratulations from all of us at the Marika Loft Gallery. You've caused quite a buzz in the art world!"

Mum stood there for a moment, baffled.

"We haven't ordered anything, thank you," she said, going to close the door.

"Mum! It's Marika's assistant! Why aren't you listening to me? I sold a painting!"

Mum looked at me and then back at Declan.

"Who *are* you?" she asked.

"I'm Declan Hewitt. Personal Assistant to Marika Loft. I would shake your hand but this is kind of heavy," said Declan, nodding towards the large box again.

"Mum? Let him in!" I pleaded. Dad joined us.

"What's going on, Cole?" he said.

"I told you!" I said. "I sold a picture and Marika Loft wants me to do another one."

Declan stepped into the house.

"Marika Loft?" said Dad. "The artist? The one who paints the boxes?"

I nodded madly.

"I'll need to take your bank details," said Declan. "Ms Loft has agreed to waive her commission on this first occasion so you'll get the full one thousand pounds."

Mum looked at Declan and then at me.

"I'm sorry … has there been some kind of mix-up?" said Mum. "Cole isn't a painter."

Declan smiled.

"Your son has a great deal of artistic talent, Mrs Miller. Marika wants to nurture that talent and has offered to manage his next sale."

"His next sale?" she said. "What do you mean?"

Declan put the box down by the stairs.

"We'd like Cole to do another painting. Marika expects his next piece to sell for more than a thousand."

Dad snorted.

"Oh, I get it!" he said. "This is some kind of practical joke, right? You've got one of those tiny cameras hidden in your button or something!"

He went over to Declan and started looking closely at his blazer.

"Dad! He's telling the truth! I *have* sold a painting!" I said. Declan was beginning to look very fed up indeed. He turned to me.

"This is all of the artists' materials that you should need, Cole," he said. "If you require anything else then just call."

I looked inside the box. There were canvases, pencils, different sized-brushes and lots and lots of paints.

"This looks perfectly satisfactory," I said, trying to sound like I knew what I was talking about. Mum and Dad just stood there until Mabel appeared and began to pull everything out of the box.

"Mabel! Hands off," said Dad. "Those are, um . . . Cole's art things."

Declan got an envelope out of his bag.

"I've got some paperwork for you to have a read through and sign, Mr and Mrs Miller."

Mum and Dad looked utterly dazed at this, but nodded in tandem, and then the three of them headed into the lounge.

"Mabel wants to see Cole's painting," whispered my little sister, beside me.

I crouched down next to her.

"Someone has bought it so you can't, I'm afraid," I said. "But I'm going to do another one!"

Mabel blinked at me with her big blue eyes.

"Sold?" she said, not really understanding what that meant.

"Yes," I said, with a big grin. "I'm going to sell the next one too!"

We followed everyone into the lounge and Mabel climbed on to Dad's lap.

"Who is that man?" she said, pointing right at Declan. She was *so* embarrassing. Dad whispered something in her ear and she went quiet.

"What kind of painting does Marika Loft want Cole to do, exactly?" said Mum. So, she finally believed me!

"Marika likes paintings that make her ask questions. Pictures with a *story*," he said earnestly. Mum nodded slowly at him and looked at me with wide eyes. I kind of shrugged back.

"And how much does she think she can sell it for?" said Dad, leaning forward.

"It's hard to say but there was a lot of interest in 'A Sky in Blue'," he said.

"Hold on a minute, is this some kind of scam?" said Dad, his eyes narrowing. "Are you going to suddenly ask us for money? To sell Cole's paintings? Because I can be very clear with you right now. We don't have any."

Declan smiled and shook his head.

"It's not a scam, Mr Miller. Cole will have the same terms as our other artists. Whatever he sells we will take thirty-five per cent to cover our gallery fees. If it doesn't sell, there's no charge. Although, to be honest with you, I think that is highly unlikely."

"Thirty-five per cent sounds like quite a chunk," said Dad.

"Yes. But remember that Marika has overheads to consider. Promotion, gallery space, insurance, staff, etc."

Dad looked at me.

"And you're sure you want to do this, Cole? You think you can do another painting?"

"Definitely!" I said.

"That's great!" said Declan, handing me a little card. "Here is my number. Please give me a call if you have any concerns."

I stared at the business card. On the front was the Loft logo in gold and on the back was a phone number and the words: *Declan Hewitt – Personal Assistant to Ms Marika Loft.*

"If I can get your signature on this contract and your bank details, Mr and Mrs Miller, I can get the thousand pounds transferred across to you this evening." He passed the form and a pen to Mum. Her face flushed.

"I could open an account for Cole, couldn't I? I mean, it feels wrong, having his money going into my account when he has done all the work."

Declan reorganized the papers in his hands. "That's between yourself and your husband, Mrs Miller. You can always move it from your account at a later date."

Mum looked at me.

"We'll talk about that later, shall we, Cole?" said Dad. I agreed, but there was no way I was keeping the money.

"We'd also like to organize a launch party at the gallery for you, Cole. A little soirée with a few journalists and other artists. It's a way of getting your art seen by a lot of people. How does that sound?"

"A swarrrr-what?" I said. I'd never heard that word before.

"A soirée," said Dad. "It's a bit like a party, but for posh people." He gave me a wink. I wasn't sure I liked the sound of that.

"How long has Cole got to do the picture?" Mum said, passing the form back.

"Within the next three weeks. Does that sound OK, Cole?"

I nodded. Considering how quickly I did the first painting, I could probably do fifty in that time.

"Great!" he said. "Please send me a photo of your work in progress to keep us updated, OK?"

"No problem," I said, making my voice sound as bright and confident as I could.

Declan stood up. "Right. I'd better be getting back to the gallery to give Marika the good news. We'll be in touch soon to see how you're getting on."

He shook my hand and then shook hands with Mum and Dad. Mabel, still in Dad's arms, held out her hand and Declan gave it a little shake as well, making her giggle.

As soon as Declan left, Mum and Dad went crazy.

"I don't believe it," said Mum. "A thousand pounds!" She squeezed me so hard I couldn't breathe and then she gave me a kiss on the top of my head.

"Who'd have thought it? Our very own artist in the family!" said Dad, hugging me as soon as Mum had let go. Mabel climbed on to the sofa and jumped up and down, clapping her hands.

Everyone started talking at once. Mum kept repeating herself about how she didn't want to take my money, but maybe they could borrow it for a while? Dad said he'd text the plumber about fixing the boiler and that, hopefully, it would then see us through the winter. Mabel jumped off of the sofa and patted me on the hand, asking if she could play with my new paints.

I stood back and smiled at everyone. I felt a warm glow growing bigger and bigger, deep inside my stomach.

I, Cole Miller, was about to make my family very, very rich.

CHAPTER FIFTEEN

Starting Painting Number Two

The next morning Mason was early for once, and he knocked for me so that we could walk to school together.

"Bye, Cole, bye, Mason!" called Dad. "Have a lovely day, you two!"

Dad was in a really good mood and Mum had also left for work with a big smile on her face. The money was in my parents' account and the plumber said he would come out and fix the boiler as soon as possible. Things were going right for us at last. The knot of worry in my tummy felt less tight, my head clearer.

"When are they going to sell your next masterpiece?" asked Mason as we walked down the road.

"In three weeks," I said. "I've got no idea what to paint though." Doing another picture had seemed really easy when Declan was round. But the more I thought about it, the more like an imposter I felt.

"You could always do a portrait of your best friend," said Mason, pulling a stupid face.

"Yeah, that's not gonna happen," I laughed.

"Why not do another sky painting? You could do a whole set of them. Lots of artists do that, don't they? Paint the same thing over and over?"

I wasn't so sure.

"I dunno," I said. "I don't think Marika would like that."

"Of course she would! When you paint 'A Sky in Blue Part 2', you might have the hump so it comes out all murky or dark or something. You could call it 'A Sky in Black'! Modern artists *love* all that rubbish."

Maybe it wasn't such a bad idea? I could even recreate my handprints on the sides. Marika seemed to like that bit. And, more importantly, it sounded easy.

"I guess so," I said, thinking it over.

Mason smirked. "The first one looked like it had been painted by a three-year-old. I think you'll be fine." He slapped me on the shoulder and laughed and I laughed back. He was right. This was going to be a piece of cake! My next painting would sell for a load of money and things at home would just get better and better.

"Have you thought about what you are going to buy when you sell your next painting?" said Mason. "You should definitely get some trainers. I'm not being funny but my gran wouldn't be seen dead in your ones."

"Yeah, I s'pose so," I said, cringing. He'd never been rude about my trainers before.

Mason went on about his XT50s and how comfortable they were but that they'd probably sold out. I'd been so busy thinking about helping Mum and Dad, I hadn't thought about buying something for myself. If my next painting sold for enough money, I might be able to get a few things for me: a new phone, a decent coat, a watch, some trainers. It would be like getting all the Christmas presents I ever wanted in one go!

When we got to form there was another message waiting for me to go and see the head teacher. "I wonder what great news he's going to give me THIS time," I said airily as I walked out, Niall and Leyton staring suspiciously after me. When I got to his office, Mr Taylor was grinning again.

"How are you today, Cole?" he asked.

"I'm great!" I said, grinning back.

"Fantastic," he said, rubbing his hands together. "I have some more good news! Marika Loft believes that Crowther High has the potential to nurture further artists, such as yourself. Isn't that incredible?"

I nodded.

"And even better than that, she has personally pledged a *substantial* sum of money to refurbish our art block! It is an incredibly generous offer, and one that we couldn't possibly have hoped for without your influence, Cole."

"Right," I said.

Mr Taylor leant forward on to his elbows.

"We *really* want you to do well with this second painting, Cole. You will be showing the whole world what *incredible* talent we have here at Crowther High. Marika said she has some big plans to get the maximum attention for your work. It's terribly exciting."

I fidgeted in my seat. "Attention?" I said. I suddenly felt really hot. Mr Taylor ignored me.

"I've had a discussion with your form tutor, and some of your teachers, and we are all in agreement that you should have the option to skip a few classes. This will enable you to have more time for your art work."

I swallowed. "Skip classes?" Mr Taylor nodded.

"Your art teacher, Mrs Frampton, said that you can make a start in her room this morning. She doesn't have any lessons until after lunch. How does that sound?"

"Um..."

"She's got all the materials you need and she can offer you advice. You can also work there during breaks and after school, if you wish. OK?"

I swallowed again. I'd gone from getting time off lessons to having to stay longer. This wasn't great.

"I guess so," I said.

"Wonderful!" said Mr Taylor, clapping his hands together. I quickly pictured my timetable in my head. I'd miss maths and French, which wasn't so bad.

"Right, get yourself off to the art room, young man, and get going on your next masterpiece!"

He stood up and reached his hand across his desk. The only time the head teacher shook hands with students was during the end-of-year assembly when he was handing out certificates. I stood up and shook it.

"We're all incredibly proud of you here, Cole," he said, his face beaming. "Very proud indeed."

I looked back at him and tried to smile, but it came out a bit wonky.

When I got to the art room, Mrs Frampton was waiting for me by her desk.

"Cole! Isn't this wonderful?" she said. She blinked madly like she did when she got really excited about something. She took a deep breath, her eyes batting open and shut.

"Do you know, I always thought you had an incredible talent deep down inside of you, Cole," she said, putting her head on one side. "I remember when I saw your woodland collage at the beginning of term. You have something *really* special." Her eyes flickered towards the back of the class and I followed her gaze. My collage had appeared on the wall with a bold label positioned underneath:

"A Woodland Scene"
by our exceptional artist, Cole Miller

All the other paintings on that wall by the year eleven GCSE students had been taken down.

"Oh," I said. "I thought you gave me a D for that?" I remembered she'd written on the back in red pen that I'd been "too heavy-handed with the glue".

Mrs Frampton closed her eyes and pursed her lips, shaking her head from side to side.

"No, no, no... It was an A-star," she said, doing a little sniff. "I've cleared an area for you, which you can use whenever you want. You won't be disturbed."

She pointed to a table in the corner covered in newspaper. On it was an easel, a selection of paints and brushes, a jam jar of water and a blank canvas. I walked towards it and put my bag down by the chair.

"I guess I'll get started, then," I said to her. She nodded and watched me intently. I rolled up my jumper sleeves and stared at the white board. The paints were all brand new. I unscrewed the top of one and squeezed it on to a plastic tray. I decided to do "A Sky in Grey".

"Oh... What an interesting choice of colour. So atmospheric, the hue of an overcast day, the threat of a storm building..." mused Mrs Frampton. I frowned at her.

"I don't think I can channel my genius if you're watching," I said.

"Of course not!" she said. "I'll just be over here if you need any... um... help." She backed up towards her desk. I twisted the easel around so that she couldn't see what I was doing and stared at the blank board. Then I took a deep breath, and began to paint.

CHAPTER SIXTEEN

First Disaster

I worked on 'A Sky in Grey' for two hours.

I started by painting the whole canvas the same colour as the elephant in Mabel's butterfly game. Then I did some white lines criss-crossing the board like the aeroplane vapour trails in 'A Sky in Blue'. While the picture was still wet I picked it up, placing my hands on the sides. I wanted to make two handprints, just like before. (I think Marika particularly like that bit.) But this time the paint smeared. They didn't look like hands at all.

When I showed Mrs Frampton, her face dropped.

"Oh," she said. "It's a bit like your first painting, isn't it? But not as ... um ... blue."

It was a mess. There was no way it would sell for fifty pence, let alone thousands.

"It's rubbish!" I said. "I can't do it!"

"Don't be silly. This is your first attempt! There's no need to panic!" said Mrs Frampton, her voice going all high. "You can't rush art."

The bell went for lunch and I threw my brush into the pot of water, grabbed my bag and headed to the door.

"Come back after school, Cole, and try again with a fresh canvas," called Mrs Frampton.

I ignored her and closed the door behind me.

"Hi, Cole! How's the painting going?" It was Isla. She must have been waiting for me.

"Badly. I just can't seem to do it right." Isla trotted beside me, trying not to crash into anyone as the corridors got busier.

"I know how you feel," she said. "I sometimes feel like that about my music compositions, when the melody just won't flow. We both have these talents but sometimes they can just desert us temporarily, can't they?"

I glanced at her but didn't say anything. I wasn't anything like Isla, was I? She carried on talking.

"Anyway, I wanted to talk to you about 'An Enigma in Oil'. I've been thinking and..."

Leyton appeared and stood in front of us, blocking our way.

"Hey, look at this," he said to Niall. "Mozart is hanging out with Picasso!"

They both laughed.

"Where's your double bass, eh, Mozart?" said Niall. A few other kids crowded around.

"Actually, it's not a double bass, it's a cello," said Isla loftily. I groaned. Answering them back was the worst thing she could do.

"Oh, is it, *actually*?" said Leyton. We tried to go around them, but a boy from year ten stopped me.

"Lend us a fiver, will ya, Picasso? We've all heard about your painting selling for a grand." Everyone laughed again.

"A grand?" said Niall. "My dad earns that within *hours*. Although, I guess that's a lot of money in your house, eh?"

I kept my head down.

"Maybe you should buy some new shoes with it," whispered a girl I didn't know.

Everyone stared down at my feet. My big toe was bursting through the end of the left shoe and I tried to make it shrink back inside, but there wasn't any room.

"At least you can afford to come on the school trips now, eh, Cole?" said Kiki, appearing behind me. I think she was trying to be kind but it wasn't helping.

"How about the skiing trip next year?" said Archie. "Do you reckon you can come on that? You're the only one not going, aren't you?"

I shrugged.

"He can't afford a ski trip after paying his dad's wages!" said Leyton. "Don't you remember? His dad's 'job' is looking after him!"

Everyone fell about laughing.

"Leave him alone!" said Isla. "Cole can't help it if he hasn't got much money."

There was a moment of silence and then we faced a machine-gun fire of insults.

"Wind it in, eh, Mozart?"

"Yeah, haven't you got orchestra practice or something?"

"Ah, does Picasso need Mozart to fight his battles for him?"

"I heard his painting looked like something a toddler could do!"

There was a gap in the crowd and I put my head down and pushed my way through.

Isla caught up with me.

"Why did you stick up for me?" I demanded. "You made it worse!"

"That's what friends do!" said Isla. "Anyway, they're just idiots. Ignore them."

I walked a bit faster and Isla stumbled as she tried to keep up.

"So, I've been thinking about the last clue in 'An Enigma in Oil' and thought that we could—"

"I really don't have time to go solving treasure hunts now, Isla," I said. "I've got to get this painting done. It's silly to go looking for treasure that might not even exist when I could be making *real* money."

Isla's face fell and she began to chew on her bottom lip. I felt a pang of guilt; I didn't want to upset her.

"OK. I'll see you later," she said, before scurrying into the canteen.

After my last lesson I went straight to the art room. Mrs Frampton gave me a new canvas and this time I tried making the grey a bit darker, but I couldn't get the vapour trails to look right. I went over and over the canvas until Mrs Frampton put her coat on.

"Why don't you have a rest from it now, Cole?" she said. "Come back tomorrow with a fresh head and it'll all seem better. It's only your first day."

I nodded and got up without saying anything. I

was so tired. I went out of the art room and headed down the corridor towards the main doors. Music was coming from the drama room and I peered in through the glass window of the door.

It was Isla.

She was sitting on a blue chair with a music stand in front of her and an auburn-coloured cello between her knees. Her eyes were shut and her head gently swayed from side to side as though she had been hypnotized. Her bow went back and forth in her right hand while the fingers on her left pressed on to the tops of the strings. The sound was incredible. Some notes were so low it sounded like rumbling thunder, and then Isla moved her fingers on her left hand and the music went high and soaring. Every now and then she stopped playing, but her right foot continued to tap steadily, her eyes closed. Maybe this was the bit when the other instruments in an orchestra were supposed to play.

As she came to the end of the music I stepped away from the door so that she couldn't see me. I don't know why Isla thought we both had such a special talent. From where I was standing it was only one of us.

When I got home, Dad came rushing to the door. "Cole! You'll never guess what's happened," he said. Mabel was jumping up and down beside him. "Marika Loft has won a big art award!"

"Oh, that's good," I said, not quite sure why Dad would be so excited about this.

"It's called the Turner Prize and she's only gone and mentioned you in her speech!"

"She did what?" I gasped, dropping my school bag on the floor. Dad flicked through his phone, pressed the screen and turned it to me. It was a snippet from the news. Marika Loft was standing on a stage. At the bottom of the screen it said: *Marika Loft. This year's winner of the Turner Prize*. I turned up the volume as she began to speak.

"*...have an incredible amount of talent in this country. In fact, only recently I visited my old high school and discovered an outstanding new artist. A young boy called Cole Miller...*"

The audience began to mutter excitedly amongst themselves. I felt a bit sick.

"*I have already sold one painting by this exceptionally talented young man and I am thrilled to announce, right here, that we will soon be auctioning his second piece of artwork. All enquiries can go through the Loft Gallery... I'd like to thank my personal assistant...*"

"An auction?" I said, stopping the video.

"Yes! The painting will go to the highest bidder. Isn't that great?"

"I guess so," I said. Mabel grabbed my hand.

"Cole? Play with Mabel?" she said, peering up at me. I wriggled my hand free.

"Declan called," said Dad. "He asked if you could send a photo of your work in progress as soon as you can. Oh, and a journalist from one of the national newspapers is coming here tomorrow to interview you! Marika's speech has caused quite a stir." Dad was grinning. I hadn't seen him look this happy in years.

"Why do they want to interview me?" I said. "Why can't they talk to Marika?"

"I guess they want to find out for themselves how special you are," said Dad, beaming.

I began to pick at my laces.

"What do you mean? There's nothing special about me," I said, trying to undo a tight knot.

"Of course there is!" laughed Dad. "Not everyone can sell a painting for a thousand pounds! They'll want an insight into the mind of a twelve-year-old art prodigy."

An art prodigy? That sounded weird.

Mabel grabbed my wrist and began to tug. "Mabel,

let go! You're hurting me!" I shouted. I shoved her and she bumped against the wall. Her face crumpled and she began to cry.

"Cole! Careful. What's wrong with you?" Dad said, scooping Mabel into his arms. "Say sorry!"

"Sorry," I muttered. "I'm just tired." Mabel wriggled down from Dad's arms and trotted off to the kitchen. Her grizzle hadn't lasted long.

"We are so proud of you, Cole," said Dad, smiling again. "Things are going right for this family at last."

I gave up with my lace and yanked my shoe off without undoing it. And then I ran upstairs.

The knot in my stomach had tightened again. This was the most exciting thing that had ever happened to my family. I should be enjoying it. But at the moment I felt like I was on top of a very high cliff, peering over the edge. And it looked like a long way down.

CHAPTER SEVENTEEN

The Journalist

The next day I tried a new painting: 'A Sky in Yellow'.
Once I nailed my second piece of art *then* I'd be able
to relax. Mrs Frampton gave me a fresh canvas and
I stayed in the art room all morning, at break time
and over lunch. Classes came and went, and I was
allowed to stay in the corner, working on my picture.

In the afternoon I went back to my lessons. In my
last class, geography, I sat next to Mason.

"How's it going?" he said.

"Terrible. I'm getting worse, not better," I replied.
"Everything just ends up as a swirling mess."

"Isla asked if we wanted to go back to the museum
tonight?" said Mason. "We've still got that clue to

solve, remember? *Listen to the river?*"

"I can't," I said. "There's a newspaper journalist coming to my house so I've got to go straight home."

"A journalist?" said Mason.

"Yeah. They want to ask questions about my art and stuff."

Mason thought about it for a moment.

"Maybe they want to know more about your mates too. Don't you think?" he said. "I could tell them how it feels to have a best mate who sold a painting for a thousand pounds!"

"Um. Maybe. But I reckon they'll want to know more about how I paint and what my inspirations are and—"

"I'm joking!" he said, shoving me on the arm. "But I'd better come back with you anyway. Just in case."

I liked Mason but I really didn't want him watching me being interviewed. I didn't know how to say no, though. As soon as the last bell rang he gave me a big grin.

"Ready?" he said. I sighed and nodded and we headed back to mine.

When we got there, there was a small, silver car parked on the road outside.

"Cole! Mason!" said Dad, opening the door. "We've been waiting for you. Come in, come in!"

Mason and I threw our bags on the floor and followed Dad into the lounge. A woman in a navy suit was sitting on our sofa. Mabel was standing by the armchair, looking shy.

The woman stood up when she saw us.

"Cole! I'm Cathy from the *Daily Chatter*. What an exciting time you're having!" she said, shaking my hand. I seemed to be shaking everyone's hands lately.

"Hello," I said.

"I'm Mason. Cole's best friend," said Mason. He reached around to shake her hand but she'd already turned away and sat down.

"Well, this is exciting, isn't it?" said Dad, sitting in the armchair. Mabel climbed on to his lap. Mason stood by the TV.

"It certainly is!" said Cathy, taking a small notepad out of her bag. "What an incredible moment for your family."

"I'm so sorry my wife couldn't join us," said Dad. "She works at the museum and she couldn't get away, unfortunately. They're closing down soon so she's a bit snowed under at the moment."

Cathy nodded and scribbled something down in her notebook. I took a peek at what she'd written: *Wife about to lose job.*

"That's no problem at all. It's mainly Cole I'd like to talk to," she said, looking up and turning to face me. "So, Cole. I'm going to ask you a few questions and record everything on my phone. Is that OK with everyone?"

I shrugged, Dad nodded and Mason said, "That's fine." I shot him a look and he pressed his lips together.

Cathy turned a page on her notepad and I could see a list of questions. She fiddled with her phone and then placed it on the sofa between us. It was recording.

"Let's make a start... Have you always been interested in art, Cole?" she said. Mason immediately snorted.

"Um. I quite liked it at primary school," I said. "I remember doing finger painting and stencils and things like that. It was good fun." Mason did an exaggerated sniff and I glared at him.

"And what did you think of Marika Loft? It must have been quite intimidating meeting one of the most iconic and famous artists that this country has ever seen. Especially one as elusive as Marika. What's she *really* like?" Cathy's eyes twinkled.

"She's all right, I guess," I said.

She nodded at me, waiting for me to carry on, but I didn't have anything else to say. She looked back down at her notes. Mabel twisted round on Dad's lap.

"Mabel have a biscuit?" she said, really loudly.

"Not now, Mabel," whispered Dad. She stared at me and the journalist, and then wriggled her way off Dad's lap and padded towards the kitchen.

"So, can you take me through what happened when Marika came into your art class the day you did the painting?" said Cathy. "What instructions did she give you?"

I took a breath.

"Well, she gave us all some art materials and told us we could paint what we wanted."

Mason suddenly stood forward. "Yeah! Remember she said we could paint the smell of coffee and all that weird stuff?" he said, laughing.

Cathy frowned at him.

"And did inspiration hit you straight away, Cole? Or did it take time to really get into that ... creative zone?"

Mason started giggling again. He was really beginning to get on my nerves.

"I guess it took a while," I said. "I didn't know what to do at first, and then I looked out of the window and—"

There was a clatter from the kitchen and then Mabel began to cry. It sounded like she was trying to get to the cupboard with the biscuits.

"I'm so sorry," said Dad, getting up. "I'll just be a second."

Cathy gave Dad a sweet smile as he left and Mason quickly sat in the armchair.

"A thousand pounds is a lot of money. Have you had any thoughts about what you might spend it on?" asked Cathy.

I opened my mouth but Mason butted in again. "He's getting some new trainers. Aren't you, Cole?" I glared at him.

"Ah, that's nice," said Cathy. "Expensive trainers are the thing to have at your age, I believe."

I shuffled in my seat.

"Actually, we need to get our boiler repaired so I think Mum and Dad are going to get that sorted. It keeps breaking down and—"

"Ah, I *see*," said Cathy, leaning closer. "So, the

money isn't entirely yours then? Are your parents intending to spend it on themselves?"

I shook my head.

"Not on themselves, exactly. It's just that we need—"

"I understand that your father is out of work at the moment," she said, interrupting. "Money must be incredibly tight for you all. This little windfall must be a huge help." She smiled again. I frowned back at her.

"He's not out of a job. He looks after me and my sister. His old job didn't pay enough to cover childcare so he decided to stay at home for now. He's actually trying to find a job that fits around us."

Cathy smiled. I watched as she wrote *dad unemployed* on her pad. I could sense Mason fidgeting in the armchair.

"And is there anything else that the money is going to go towards? A new carpet, perhaps?" She looked down at our old, thin carpet with the bald patches. "Some decorating?"

"We . . . we haven't decided yet," I said.

"I think it's up to Cole where the money should be spent, don't you?" said Mason, perching on the edge of the armchair. Cathy fixed him with a steely glare.

"Of course," she said. "It's just that I'm sure most twelve-year-olds would choose to spend the money on a new PlayStation or the latest phone. Not a gas boiler."

She turned back to me and her smile magically returned.

"I understand there is already a lot of interest in your next painting. Marika Loft's gallery have made a statement saying that they expect it to go for well over a thousand pounds at the auction. How does it feel to know you will be getting another large sum of money? It must be quite exciting, I imagine? Considering…" She looked around our shabby front room. "Considering you … you know … haven't got much."

Mason huffed and stood up.

"Why do you keep asking him about the money?" he said. "Shouldn't you be talking about his art?"

"I'm getting on to that next," she said, glaring at him. "Cole? How about this next sum of money? Will *you* be spending it, or your parents?"

"I … I don't know. It depends how much there is, I guess," I said. "My mum is going to get me a bank account and—"

"So, the thousand pounds isn't even in your bank account?"

I opened my mouth and closed it again. I didn't

like her questions. She looked down at her notepad and ignored the fact that I hadn't answered.

"And how is the second painting coming along?" she said. "Any hints for our readers as to what it's of?"

I felt myself turning red. "I'm not sure yet."

Cathy frowned.

"But isn't the sale in a couple of weeks?" she said. "You must be feeling *immense* pressure to produce something as good as, if not better than, your first painting?"

I blinked and looked down at my knees as I thought about what to say. I suddenly remembered what Marika had said on the phone in Mr Taylor's office.

"I'm letting the painting *speak* to me first. Then I'll begin," I said. As soon as the words had left my mouth I blushed. Mason spluttered out a loud guffaw and put his hand over his mouth. I glared at him again and then Dad came through the door with Mabel on his hip. She had a ginger biscuit in her hand and a red bump just above her eyebrow.

"How are we getting on?" asked Dad, with a smile.

"I think we're done!" said Cathy, stopping the recording on her phone. Mabel wriggled out of Dad's arms and trotted over to Cathy, standing right in front of her.

"Mabel banged her head getting a biscuit!" my

sister said proudly. Cathy stared at her, not smiling.

Undeterred, my sister went to the arm of the sofa and whacked it with the palm of her hand. "Look! Our sofa makes clouds!" she said as dust puffed into the air. I saw Cathy's eyes widen when she saw it.

"So it does," she said. She smiled and quickly wrote something down before putting her notebook into her bag. It wasn't that the sofa was dirty, it was just old. Mum and Dad bought it from a charity shop when I was little and it had been ancient even then.

"Thank you so much for your time," said Cathy, getting up. Mabel scooted out of her way and went to stand beside Dad. "Can I just get a quick photo of you, Cole? Maybe sitting in the middle of the sofa?"

"I guess," I said, looking at Dad, who nodded. I edged to the middle as Cathy crouched down and held up her phone. She spotted something behind me and repositioned herself.

"Lovely!" she said, pressing the screen. "Thank you, Cole, and thank you, Mr Miller. I know that it's an extremely exciting time for you all and I *know* that our readers will enjoy learning all about it."

"No problem," said Dad.

"I'll get this written up and it'll make tomorrow's paper," she said.

"That's wonderful," said Dad. "Thank you for coming." He went into the hallway to show her out.

When they'd gone, I got up to see what Cathy had been looking at before she took my picture. Right above me was a bare patch of wall. Dad had said the whole room needed to be plastered and then decorated, but they never had the money to get it done. It had been like that for so long I barely noticed it, but I knew it looked awful. I was pretty sure that Cathy had deliberately positioned herself so that the scruffy patch was in the picture.

"You all right?" said Mason, getting up.

"Yeah. Why wouldn't I be?" I snapped back.

"It's just that she kept asking you about the money you were getting," he said.

"She's a journalist. What else is she going to ask me?" I said. Mason turned away.

"OK. Well, I'll see you tomorrow then," he said.

I didn't answer him as I looked around our worn-out room. I had a bad feeling about Cathy's newspaper article. A very bad feeling indeed.

CHAPTER EIGHTEEN

In the Newspaper

When I walked into form the next day, everyone stopped talking and turned round to stare at me. I sat down next to Isla. There was no sign of Mason; he must have slept through his alarm again.

"What's going on?" I asked quietly. Isla frowned.

"They've been talking about your interview," she said. "The one in the newspaper."

"What about it?"

Isla took her phone out of her bag, checked that Miss Canning wasn't about to appear, then scrolled the screen. The headline made my stomach churn.

MUM AND DAD HAVE DESIGNS
ON MY MILLIONS!

Cole Miller has burst on to the art scene as the next "big new thing", but how will he spend his money? The 12-year-old art prodigy's first painting, 'A Sky in Blue', sold at the Marika Loft Gallery for an impressive £1,000. However, Ms Loft said that the young boy is destined for huge wealth, as interest increases around his next picture (as yet untitled), due to be sold at auction in a couple of weeks.

I visited Cole in his family's rundown, three-bedroomed terraced house.

"I'd like some new trainers, but my parents need the money to repair the boiler," he told me sadly. Looking around the Miller home, I can see that money appears to be exceptionally tight. I couldn't help but wonder if Cole's attempt to sell a second painting was more his parents' idea than Marika Loft's? The Loft Gallery were unavailable to comment.

I stopped reading, feeling a bit sick. I hadn't said that at all!

"Is it true?" whispered Isla. "Are your parents making you paint and taking the money?"

"No!" I said. I scrolled further down the screen and saw the photograph that she'd taken of me on our worn-out sofa. Behind me was the bare patch of plaster. I looked thoroughly miserable. Underneath it read:

"I just want some new trainers," said Cole Miller, 12.

Isla quickly put her phone back in her bag as Miss Canning walked in. Mason came rushing in behind her and dived into his seat.

"What have I missed?" he asked. Isla whispered to him while I stared at the desk. This was awful. Now everyone would think my parents were money-grabbing!

Miss Canning took the register and then we all trooped off to the hall for a whole-school assembly. We had to sit through these assemblies once a month and everyone hated them. The corridor was packed and a hand thumped me on the back.

"Is it true that you're *paying* your dad to look after you and your sister?" said Hannah. I thought she was joking, but she looked serious.

"Of course I'm not," I mumbled.

"I heard they're going to keep all the money but give you an allowance of one pound a week," said Niall, Leyton smirking beside him. "Ha! That's a pound more than you were getting before though, right, Cole?" he said.

I looked up for Mason and Isla but they were deep in conversation a few metres ahead. Probably talking about me.

"I really think you should get a manager or someone to look after your money, Cole," said Kiki. A few others tried to push closer to hear what was going on.

"My parents aren't taking my money, OK?!" I said to the crowd around me. "The newspaper was lying!"

I pushed my way through to the hall and sat between Dean and Pia. I slumped down in my seat as far as I could. The teachers were really strict in assemblies and they stalked the edges of the hall, watching for talkers. No one dared say anything else to me.

Mr Taylor began by handing out various sports trophies and awards. Isla collected two certificates. One for getting top grades in a music exam and one for a geography project she did on South America.

"What outstanding students we have in this school," said Mr Taylor, after he'd handed out the last award. "Crowther High really does have an incredible amount of talent in this hall right now..."

I fidgeted in my seat and glanced at the clock. There was still ten minutes to go. It was dragging on for ever.

"And talents can reveal themselves from a very young age, as history has shown," he continued. "Who would like to guess how old Wolfgang Amadeus Mozart was when he began composing? Anyone?"

A few people shot a look at Isla and sniggered. Three hands went up and he pointed to a boy in the middle.

"Thirty-four?" he said. Mr Taylor smiled and shook his head.

"Mozart was just five years old when he began creating music. Isn't that incredible?" he said. No one reacted. We were all just waiting for assembly to be over.

"And I'm delighted to say that Crowther High has its very own 'Mozart', but this time from the art world. Where are you, Cole Miller?"

I squirmed in my seat as every head turned to me.

"Could you stand up, please?" Mr Taylor called, stretching his neck to try and find me. I kept my head down but slowly rose to my feet.

"Ah! There he is. I'm sure many of you know that Cole has already sold a painting at the renowned Marika Loft Gallery. He is currently working on his second piece, which will be sold soon at auction, isn't that right, Cole?"

I nodded, not looking up. There was no way I was going to actually say anything.

"And because of Cole's amazing artistic abilities, Marika Loft has decided to invest in our art department to help nurture the talents of our students. Could we all give Cole a big round of applause?"

I glanced up and saw the teachers around the edge of the hall smiling at me and clapping enthusiastically. The kids around me just slapped their hands together and a couple of them yawned. I waited a few seconds then sat down, sliding in my chair as low as I could. Mr Taylor read a few notices about some sporting events coming up in the school calendar and then assembly was over.

"Oohh, get Picasso," said Archie as we all filed out to first lesson. "Who's the next big thing, eh?"

Everyone started laughing until one of the teachers

told them to be quiet. I spent the rest of the day trying to smile and laugh along with everyone's comments, but it got really tiring. Mrs Frampton stopped me in the corridor.

"Cole! Are you painting in my class later? I have a few ideas if you wanted my help at all?"

A few students hung around, waiting to hear what I'd say.

"I can't tonight. I'm busy," I said. The truth was, I couldn't face staring at another blank canvas.

When I got in from school, Mum was already home. She and Dad were in the kitchen. Dad jumped when I walked in, so I guessed they'd been talking about me.

"Cole!" said Dad, looking over Mum's shoulder. "How was school? All OK?"

"Yep, all good," I said, even though it had been a pretty awful day.

There was a copy of the *Daily Chatter* on the kitchen table. They must have seen Cathy's article.

"We need to talk to you, darling," said Mum. "Your father and I have discussed it and we have decided that you should keep all the money from your first painting. We're going to open an account for you this week."

"What? But that's stupid! The boiler needs fixing, the house needs decorating..." I shouted. "And you're going to be out of a job soon. Then what will we do?"

Dad sighed.

"But it's not our money to spend," he said. "It's yours."

I folded my arms. "Well, in that case *I* will pay for the boiler to be fixed."

Mum smiled. "That's really sweet of you, Cole, but we've made our decision. They said in the paper that—"

"I don't care what the newspaper people say, it's *my* money and it's up to me what I do with it. And I choose that it is spent on things at home. OK?"

Mum was about to try and hug me but I took a step back. She looked at Dad.

"It *would* help us out, Jenny," he said. "Perhaps we can pay him back?"

"Doug, I'm going to be unemployed in a few weeks' time. How are we going to do that?"

"That's even more reason to use the money, then!" I said.

Mum looked between us.

"And anyway," I said, "my next painting is going to sell *way* more than the first. You saw what Marika said in the paper, didn't you? 'Destined for huge wealth'. That's what she said about me! We're going to be rich!"

Mum took a breath and laughed.

"I guess if the next painting goes for more, then Cole can have most of it," she said.

"What do you mean *if*?" I laughed. "It's going to sell for a fortune!"

Dad laughed too then. "That's the spirit! This family is due some good luck at last!" he said.

"We could get the washing machine looked at," said Mum, her eyes shining. "It keeps getting stuck on spin. And you need a new mattress, Cole, and we could maybe get a rug to go over the carpet in the lounge. I hate that carpet."

"We should definitely get the lounge decorated," I said, thinking of the photo in the paper. "That's got to be at the top of the list. *And* we all need some smart clothes to wear to the gallery. Something posh."

Dad put his arm around Mum. They seemed taller than usual, like they could float up to the ceiling. It was like a huge, heavy burden had been taken off their shoulders.

"Thank you, Cole," Mum said. The two of them squeezed me into a big hug. My stomach churned as I shut my eyes. I wanted to tell them that I was worrying. That I wasn't sure I'd be able to paint anything at all. But I couldn't quite find the right words.

CHAPTER NINETEEN

The Pressure is On

For the next week and a half I went into school an hour early, worked through every break time, and stayed for an hour after normal lessons had finished. By the end of the week I had sent three photos to Declan: 'A Sky in Pink', 'A Sky in Red' and 'A Sky in Green'. Declan messaged back after each one saying Marika didn't think they were quite right.

Marika said to forget your first painting and try something new. Paint from the heart.

I didn't reply and it wasn't long before he became suspicious.

If you need more time, Cole, then please
let me know immediately. The launch is just
days away. It would be extremely awkward
if we have nothing to auction. Declan

I quickly typed my reply.

No, it's all fine! It's coming along great! It
has lots of heart and asks lots of questions!
I'll send you a photo asap! Cole

On Wednesday, after school I was back in the art
room. The auction was three days away.

"Cole, I've been thinking," said Mrs Frampton
from behind her desk. "Why don't we call Ms Loft
and tell her that you're having a bit of trouble finding
your feet with this painting? I'm sure she would
understand if you need more time."

I didn't look up as I pressed my brush on to the
board, a pile of ruined canvases beside me.

Mrs Frampton didn't understand. Time was
something I didn't have. The museum was shutting
down soon and we needed the money. Fast.

I shook my head.

"It's fine. This one is going to be much better," I

said. "I'm trying something different." I put my brush down and took a pace back. Mrs Frampton got up and stood beside me. This time I'd tried to paint a jug that had been on a shelf in the art room. It looked more like a giant jelly baby.

"I just don't think it's working, Cole. I think... I think there's too much pressure on you and I think you're trying too hard."

"I'm not trying too hard," I snapped back. I picked up my brush and began to paint again. What did she know? She was just a stupid art teacher. Marika hadn't even taken any notice of her when she came to our school!

Mrs Frampton stood there for a while, then went back to her desk. I painted a few more strokes before I threw down my brush and grabbed my bag. I'd had enough.

"Remember what I said, Cole," called Mrs Frampton. "You can ask for more time. It doesn't mean you're giving in!"

"I'm fine, Miss," I said, and I closed the door behind me.

When I got home, Dad asked if I could look after Mabel while he popped out to buy something smart to wear for the auction. Mum had already ordered some clothes for me. They were still unopened in my bedroom.

"How's the painting?" he said.

I gave him the biggest smile I could. "Great!" I said. "I'm really pleased with it."

Dad smiled and placed his hand on my arm.

"That's terrific, Cole," he said. "We're so very proud of you, you know."

There was a clatter upstairs. It sounded like Mabel was in my bedroom.

"You'd better make sure she's not going through those paints that Declan brought round," said Dad, putting his denim jacket on. "I caught her in your room earlier."

I watched him putting his phone and keys into his jacket pocket. The urge to say something was overwhelming. I wanted to grab him tightly around his waist and tell him. To tell him that I couldn't do the painting and that I had let them all down. I took a deep breath as Dad turned to me.

"Thanks, son," he said. "You've really given this family hope. We'll never forget it." He ruffled my hair and opened the front door. As it closed behind him I ran upstairs. Mabel was sitting on my carpet with a canvas on the floor in front of her. She had an open tube of red paint in one hand and one of grey in the other.

"Mabel! What are you doing?!" I shouted.

"Making pictures like Cole!" she said, with a huge smile.

"No!" I shouted. "Those paints are really expensive. They're not yours to play with. Put them down, NOW!"

Mabel looked at me. She looked at the tubes of paint in her hands, and at the fresh, blank canvas on the floor. The temptation was just too much. She took a little breath then squeezed. Two lumps of red and grey paint splatted on to the board. We both stared at them. Mabel rested the tubes on the cardboard lid of the box, then pressed her fingers into the blobs. She slowly swirled the paint up and down, making two long oblong shapes on each side of the canvas.

"Mabel! Stop!" I said. "You're making a mess!" She ignored me and began to pitter-patter her little fingers all over the canvas like tiny raindrops.

"Aren't you listening?" I said. "You're not supposed to touch things that don't belong to you. Mum and Dad are going to be so angry when I tell them!"

She looked at me, and then back at her picture.

"This is Cole," she said, pointing to the large, red

blob. "And this is Mabel." She pointed to the grey blob. "We're catching the butterflies!"

I stared at the canvas. She was painting a picture of us playing her favourite game. The little dots that she had made with her fingertips were butterflies, not raindrops.

"Cole play the butterfly game now?" she said. If there was one thing I really, really didn't want to do, it was play that stupid game.

"Look, if you're really, *really* careful then you can finish the picture, OK?"

My little sister's lips curled up and her eyes twinkled. She grabbed a brush from the box.

"Wait and I'll fetch some newspaper so you don't get paint on the carpet," I said. "Don't touch *anything.*" I quickly ran downstairs, got the *Daily Chatter* from the kitchen table, then went back to my room and spread it on the floor. I put Mabel's painting on top.

"Cole do a painting too?" she said, moving her brush on the board.

"I can't. I've tried, but I just can't do it again," I said. "I've let everybody down, Mabel. Marika, the school, Mum, Dad, you ... everyone. They all think I'm special, but I'm not."

As I watched my little sister paint as if she didn't have a care in the world, I could feel all the worry bubbling up to the back of my throat. A tear ran down my cheek and I quickly wiped it away.

"Marika Loft has made a really big mistake," I continued. "I'm not an art prodigy. That painting was just a fluke. I won't have anything to take to the auction and everyone will know the truth. That I'm just one big fake. Mum will lose her job at the museum and we won't have any money and..."

I didn't finish my sentence. The thought of Mum being unemployed made me really want to sob, and I didn't want to do that in front of Mabel. But she was too absorbed in her painting to notice. She sat back and dropped the paint-covered brush on to the newspaper.

"Do you know what, Mabel?" I said, sniffing away my tears. "That's actually quite good."

The colours were bright and clear and it wasn't obvious what it was, so it definitely made you want to ask questions. Mabel picked the brush up again and gently dabbed it on the canvas, adding two wonky triangle shapes next to the larger blobs that were our bodies.

"Are those the nets for the butterflies?" I asked. Mabel nodded. She did a few more strokes but it wasn't long before she became more interested in the paint on her fingers than the paint on the board.

"Come on. We'd better clean you up," I said, putting the lids back on to the tubes.

She watched me as she sat cross-legged on my carpet. There were little flecks of dried paint all over her leggings.

"Mummy and Daddy might tell Mabel off," she said, looking at me and then at the picture.

"I can hide it under my bed if you like?" I said. "It can be our little secret. How about that?"

She grinned and put her finger to her lips.

"Ssshhhh," she said. She shuddered with the excitement of having a secret between just the two of us and then she suddenly grabbed the painting and held it up.

"Mind out, Mabel! You're covered in paint. You'll ruin it," I said. She put the picture back down, leaving half of a red handprint in one corner.

"Oh," she said sadly. "My hand went splodge."

"It doesn't matter," I said. "It's still good. Go to the bathroom and I'll help you clean up." She jumped up and skipped to the landing. I took another long look at her painting and then I slid it underneath my bed where no one would see it.

CHAPTER TWENTY

Copying Van Gogh

When we sat down to dinner that evening, Mum gave us a sneak preview of the dress she'd bought for the auction. Even the carrier bag was posh and made of thick, glossy paper with white cord handles. She took the dress out and held it up against herself as she swished around the kitchen. It was dark green and shimmered as it caught the light.

"Ooohhh," said Mabel, staring.

"It looks lovely, Mum," I said, pushing my dinner to the side of the plate. I really wasn't hungry.

Mum smiled and put the dress back in the bag.

"Declan said they are going to send a car with a chauffeur," said Mum. "A chauffeur! For us!"

"Really?!" said Dad and they both started giggling like a couple of kids. I smiled along and then pushed my plate away and stood up.

"I'm going to go and finish my painting now," I said, trying to sound cheery.

Mum sat back in her chair.

"Oh, have you got it here?" she said. "Can we see it?"

"Ah, not yet!" I said, smiling as if it was all just a joke. "It's not finished yet!" *It's not even started,* I said to myself in my head. Mum and Dad laughed and Mabel joined in too, even though she probably didn't know why.

When I got to my room I picked out a canvas from the box of art materials that Declan had left and spread more of the newspaper out on my floor.

This was it. Time had run out. Declan had texted me to say they needed to see a photo by tomorrow morning or they'd call the whole thing off. Whatever I painted now would have to be good enough to be auctioned on Saturday.

I looked around for inspiration. In the corner of my room was an old wooden chair. I never sat on it; I just used it to put my dirty clothes on. I remembered learning about Vincent Van Gogh in primary school and I was sure that he had painted a picture of a chair. He also did lots of paintings of bright yellow sunflowers and one of a sapphire-blue sky filled with twinkly stars. I liked those pictures. He was quite ill and cut his own ear off. I remember we all went really quiet in class when we heard about that. Apparently, he died without ever knowing how loved his paintings were.

I searched for the Van Gogh painting on my phone. He had painted a pipe on his chair. I swept the dirty clothes off of my chair and placed a tennis ball on the seat. Me and Dad used to play catch with that ball over at the Sideway playing fields before they built flats there.

I sat on the floor, took a deep breath and began.

After two hours I took a look at my final picture. The piece of art that everyone was counting on to make us a lot of money. The legs on the chair were wonky and the green paint of the ball had run into the brown of the seat. I went over and over the paint, but the more I tried, the more of a mess it became. I felt tears stream down my face, but then I heard someone coming along the hall and I quickly wiped them away.

There was a quiet tap and Mum appeared around

the door. "I've just put Mabel to bed," she said. "How's it going?"

"Fine," I lied, quickly getting up and blocking her view. "Don't look. I don't want you to see it until it's finished."

"OK, but make sure you send a photograph to Declan first thing tomorrow, won't you?"

I nodded but didn't say anything. I tried smiling at her but it was hard when I felt all scrunched up inside. I was tempted to just tell her the truth: that the first painting had been pure luck and Marika had seen something in it that I hadn't intended and couldn't repeat. I wanted to say that I hated painting and I never wanted to do it ever again. But Mum was about to lose her job. We would soon have no money and lots of bills to pay and everyone was relying on me. I couldn't give up now.

"Do another hour and then take a break, Cole. Promise me?" she said.

"I promise," I said, and she quietly closed my door.

An hour later I put my paintbrush down. I'd managed to make the tennis ball look more like a circle, but I just couldn't get the chair legs to look right. They were still crooked in places, but they'd have to do. What would Marika think? Would she still think I was *an outstanding new artist*? I seriously doubted it.

I slid the picture carefully beneath my bed and went downstairs. Dad had fallen asleep on the sofa and Mum was watching a wildlife programme about penguins.

"Want to watch this with me for a bit?" she said. I looked at the screen. There was a snow blizzard and a huddle of penguins stood motionless as the wind howled around them. A grey baby penguin appeared to be lost. It was battling against the wind as it slowly walked around a huddle of adults, calling for its mum. The other penguins already had their babies, tucked snugly between their feet. The young chick went around the group, opening its little beak and saying, "Chur-chirp! Chur-chirp!" to each and every bird. But the heads of the big penguins hung low against the swirling snow.

"I think I'll go to bed," I said. "I'm really tired."

Mum turned to me.

"OK, darling," she said. "I'm really proud of you, you know? I know you've found the past couple of weeks a bit stressful, but you've done so well. You should be so proud."

"Thanks, Mum," I said. She turned back to the TV. I watched as the baby penguin drifted from adult to adult, but not one turned to help it.

*

That night I dreamt I was standing alone on a frozen wasteland. I looked down and all I had on were my pyjamas. I folded my arms against the cold as my bare feet wriggled against the icy snow. Around me was a vast expanse of white, just like a blank canvas. I turned and saw a small, dark shape coming towards me. I couldn't make out what it was, but it was making a sound. It appeared to be saying something.

"I can't hear you! You'll have to shout!" I yelled as the thing got closer and closer.

I turned my head to one side, trying to listen. The shape staggered closer, struggling to walk against the wind. And then I heard it.

"Chur-chirp! Chur-chirp!"

It was the baby penguin. I ran towards it, stumbling in the freezing snow and ice.

"Don't worry! I'll help you!" I shouted above the roar of the wind. I dug my feet into the ice, but no matter how fast I ran, the baby penguin was just too far away. I couldn't get any closer. I tried one more step and slipped, falling face down into the snow.

I jolted awake and shivered. My duvet had fallen on to the floor and my bedroom was icy cold. I rolled over and switched my lamp on, and then I reached down for my covers. A corner of my canvas jutted out from under my bed. I eased it out to take another look and see if it was as bad as I feared, but it wasn't my painting, it was Mabel's: the one of us playing the butterfly game. I stared at the picture, and then I slid it back beneath my bed.

CHAPTER TWENTY-ONE

Sending a Photo to Declan

There was a knock at the front door at 8.15 a.m. I heard Dad's voice.

"Oh hello, Mason. Go on up."

My painting was on the floor in the middle of my room and I heard Mason thump up the stairs.

"Is that it?" he said, coming in. "A chair? What happened to 'A Sky in Beige' or whatever?"

"Marika didn't like that one," I muttered.

Mason crouched down and examined my painting.

"It's not bad, I guess," he said. "I don't think I'd pay a fiver for it but ... you know. Who can argue with other people's weird tastes?"

I knew he was trying to make me laugh, but I

wasn't in the mood for jokes. I'd only had a few hours sleep and I was so worried that Marika would reject it. If she did, well, that was it. No auction and no money. Mabel suddenly appeared in my doorway.

"Hello, Mabel," said Mason, grinning at her. "How are you?"

Mabel went shy and dropped her head. She bounded across the room and stood beside me, putting her little hand on my shoulder as I fiddled with my phone.

"Mabel got *allllllll* messy!" she said.

"You got messy? How did that happen then?" said Mason. His voice went high when he talked to Mabel. I don't think he found it easy to talk to little kids.

"I did a picture and I got paint ALL on my fingers!" she said, wiggling her hands at him. He laughed. "My hand went SPLODGE!" she said, smacking her hand on to her leg like she had with the red paint on to the canvas.

"You'll have to show me your picture one day," he said. "I'd like that."

Mabel did three little jumps and my floorboards creaked as she dropped to her knees with a thump. "It's *here*!" she said in a hushed voice. She dived under my bed and reappeared with her painting.

"Shhhhh," she said. "It's a secret. Mummy and Daddy said don't touch Cole's paints 'cos he's doing something very 'portant."

Mason smiled at her.

"Oh, Mabel. That's brilliant," said Mason. "I actually think it's better than Cole's, don't you?"

Mabel looked at mine and then back at hers and nodded. Mason laughed.

"That's me and that's Cole," she said, pointing at the shapes. "We're playing the butterfly game!"

"Right..." said Mason, not having a clue what she was on about. Mabel's confidence was growing now and she jumped up and grabbed Mason's hand.

"Come and see the butterfly game!" she said, pulling him along.

"OK. But we've got to leave for school in a minute," he said as Mabel dragged him out of my room.

I looked down at the paintings on my bedroom floor and then I realized I hadn't added my signature. I grabbed a brush from the art box and squeezed a tiny blob of dark blue paint on to the end. I stared at it for a moment, took a deep breath, then carefully painted a curly "C" in the bottom left-hand corner. I found my phone, took a picture and forwarded it to Declan, before sliding the two pictures back under my bed.

CHAPTER TWENTY-TWO

'Catch' by Cole Miller

All day long I fretted about the picture. What if Marika hated it? Would they call the auction off? What would happen then? Although I knew exactly what would happen. Mum's job would come to an end and we wouldn't have any money in the bank.

I tried to take a peek at my phone during chemistry to see if Declan had replied, but I nearly got caught. I didn't want my phone confiscated so I shoved it to the bottom of my bag and tried to forget about it. I'd just have to wait until the end of the day.

As soon as the last bell rang I grabbed my stuff and ran out of class. I pushed the heavy door open and went into the playground.

"Cole! Can you come to the museum today? I need to talk to you about the next clue." It was Isla. She must have run after me. I'd completely forgotten about 'An Enigma in Oil'; finding that note in the canopic jar felt like a lifetime ago.

"Sorry, Isla," I said, turning my phone on. "I'm busy tonight."

I stared at my phone as it lit up and put in my security code. When I looked up, Isla had gone. I felt a bit bad, but I had enough things going on at the moment. Most crucially whether Marika liked the painting.

A message flashed on to the screen.

> You've done it, Cole! I love it. It's a painting from the heart and it really tells a story. Well done! Declan will collect it today. What is the title? We'll do a grand unveiling just before the auction. Marika.

I grinned and did a little air punch. She *loved* it! A huge wave of relief washed through me. Everything was going to be OK. I quickly thought up a title and texted back.

I'm pleased you like it! It's called 'Catch'.
Why aren't you showing the picture before
the auction? Cole

There was a beep as her message arrived.

To create a bit of drama! Trust me. People
will flock to view 'Catch' by Cole Miller for
the very first time. M.

That made me nervous. What if they revealed the painting at the auction and everybody laughed? My stomach somersaulted. I just had to hope that Marika knew what she was doing.

When I got home, Dad came to the door. He was grinning from ear to ear.

"Cole! Guess what! The boiler is fixed. We have hot water at last!" He gave me a hug and I squeezed him back.

"That's great, Dad," I said.

"The plumber said we'd need to replace the whole system at some point, but it should see us through the winter." He kissed the top of my head and I took my coat off.

"Oh, and Declan rang and said he'd be here in half an hour to get the painting. Can I have a look before it goes?"

"Um. No," I said. "Marika wants to reveal it at the auction."

Dad frowned.

"But I'm not bidding on it, am I?" He laughed. "I'm your dad and I'd like to take a look before my famous son gets even more famous!"

He ruffled my hair. I hated it when he did that. Mabel appeared at the top of the stairs and started to come down. She had a butterfly net in her hand.

"Butterfly game!" she said. I groaned.

"Can you have a word with her?" I said, kicking off my shoes. "She keeps pestering me to play that stupid game all the time."

Dad looked at me.

"Are you all right?" he said.

"Yes," I snapped. "I just don't understand why you want to see the painting when the *whole* point is that there's going to be this big reveal on Saturday. That's all."

I ran upstairs. I thought Dad might come and knock on my door, but he must have decided it was best to leave me to it, and before long I could hear him clattering about getting dinner ready.

After about half an hour I heard Declan arrive. I quickly got down on to my knees, pulled the painting from underneath my bed and stared at it. This was it. There was no going back now. I went out on to the landing and listened to them talking.

"I understand that Marika wants the painting to be a surprise?" said Dad.

"Yes, Mr Miller. The painting will only be revealed moments before the auction begins. It's great publicity for the Marika Loft Gallery and for Cole."

"He won't even show me!" said Dad, laughing nervously. "But you're the experts, so I guess you know what you're doing."

I began to make my way down with the painting under my arm. Mabel scooted out from the kitchen.

"You've got big eyebrows," she said to Declan. He laughed, casually wiping the back of his hand across his forehead. My sister was *so* embarrassing.

"Right, well we'd better get out of the way in case we see the painting and ruin the surprise, eh, Mabel?" said Dad, taking my little sister's hand. "Thanks for coming to pick it up, Declan. We'll see you at the auction tomorrow." They headed to the kitchen and

I ran downstairs. Declan held out a black cloth bag and I carefully placed the painting inside.

"Thanks, Cole. It's absolutely terrific. I think it is going to create a huge buzz throughout the art world. This is going to be the biggest and best night of your young life!" said Declan. "Right, I'd better get back to the gallery so that we can get set up." He opened the door and then turned back to me.

"We'll see you at the auction, Cole," he said, patting me on the side of the arm. "And well done again."

"Thanks," I croaked. "See you there."

I closed the door behind him and took a deep breath.

I went to bed early that night. Mum popped into my room to see if the clothes she'd ordered fit me OK. She'd chosen a blue cotton shirt and dark navy trousers with a pair of smart, black shoes. I said they were all fine, even though I hadn't tried them on. I turned away and stared at the wall.

"Is everything OK, Cole?" said Mum. I felt my mattress sag as she sat down on the end of my bed. "I can't wait to see your painting. It'll be a nice surprise for us as well as everybody else. I'm sure you're nervous but you've got nothing to worry about.

Marika is clearly very impressed."

We were quiet for a moment and then I rolled on to my back.

"Mum? Can Mabel stay here when we go to the auction?"

"Stay here? Why?" said Mum.

I sat myself up.

"She's too young and it's going to be a really late night and ... and, well, she's so embarrassing. Did Dad tell you what she said about Declan's eyebrows?"

Mum smiled.

"Cole, she's three years old. I think that excuses her a little bit, don't you?" she said.

"But she'll just show us all up," I said. "*Please*, Mum?"

"We can't leave her out, Cole. It wouldn't be fair. This is a once-in-a-lifetime event for *all* of us. She'll want to be there just as much as we do."

I didn't say anything.

"I've got a little surprise that might cheer you up," she said, smiling. "I had a word with Declan and Mason can come along with us."

"Mason?!" I said. Mum frowned.

"I thought it would be nice for you to have your best friend there," she said. "What's wrong with

Mason coming?"

I kept quiet.

Mum put her hand on my arm, but I shuffled down under the duvet, bringing it up to my neck.

"What's wrong, Cole? Are you getting nervous?" she said.

I shrugged. "I just don't want my embarrassing sister there," I said, glaring at my duvet.

"Well, she's coming and that's the end of it," said Mum. "I'm sorry if you're ashamed of your sister, Cole. I'm pretty sure that she doesn't feel the same way about you."

And with that, she reached towards my lamp and switched it off. I turned over and curled up in the darkness. Falling asleep felt impossible. Every time I closed my eyes I saw the painting and imagined everybody pointing and laughing after the big reveal. Or could it be possible that Marika was right and everyone would love it? I bounced from one thought to another and my head began to ache. One thing was for certain though: after Saturday nothing would be the same again.

CHAPTER TWENTY-THREE

The Marika Loft Gallery

It was Saturday afternoon, the day of the auction. Our car was arriving at five to take us to London. It was 4.55 p.m. and there was no sign of Mason.

"Can't you call him and find out where he is?" said Mum. "It would be a shame for him to miss it."

I got my phone out of my trouser pocket.

"Too late. The car's here!" said Dad, looking out of the window for the hundredth time.

Mum and I rushed over to take a look. It was silver with sliding doors and blacked-out windows. A man in a suit and wearing dark glasses got out and headed towards the house.

"Don't let him see us staring!" said Mum, giggling

as she fell back on to the sofa. She was wearing her new dress with a silky shawl over her shoulders. She looked really lovely. Dad was wearing a pair of navy trousers and a shirt a bit like mine, but he had a smart jacket over the top. The last time I'd seen Mabel she was wearing a white dress and a pair of sparkly silver shoes, which were now discarded on the sofa. There was a knock on the door and Mum let out a little high-pitched squeak.

"It's the driver! Where's Mabel?" she said, grabbing her shoes. "Come on, Mabel! We've got to go!"

Mabel came thumping down the stairs. She'd taken off her dress and was wearing her old denim dungarees over a stripy top. One of the shoulder straps was undone and there was a big orange stain down the front.

"See what I mean, Mum?" I cried. "She can't come looking like that!"

Mabel ignored me and sat on the bottom step, stuffing her little feet into the silver shoes. She clearly still liked that part of her outfit. Mum sighed.

"Where's your lovely dress, Mabel?" she said. "Why have you taken it off?"

"There isn't time to change her now," said Dad, grabbing his door keys. "Cole, text Mason and tell him we've had to go without him."

Mum opened the front door.

"Good evening, ma'am," said the chauffeur. "I'm Nick, your driver. If you'd all like to follow me, we can be on our way."

Mum turned to me and grinned, her cheeks flushed.

Mabel was the first to get in the car. There was a booster seat all ready for her by the window. Mum climbed in beside her and Dad sat in the front next to Nick. I got in behind Mum and Mabel and fiddled with my seatbelt. A face suddenly appeared at my window and someone tapped on the glass.

"Sorry I'm late!" It was Mason. He climbed into the back and sat next to me. His cheeks were bright red from running.

"I didn't think you were going to make it," I said.

"What?" he said, grinning. "I wouldn't miss this for the world."

He pulled his seatbelt across his chest and clicked it into place.

"I'm ready!" he called to Nick, who was back in the driving seat. The car slowly pulled away and I looked out at our scruffy, cold house and crossed my fingers.

After two hours of driving, we pulled up outside a large white building. Above the door in small, silver letters it read: *The Marika Loft Gallery*.

"Here we are, everybody," called Nick.

"It looks so smart," whispered Mum.

A small crowd of people stood behind a red rope at the side of entrance. A few of them were drinking out of takeaway coffee cups and they had expensive-looking cameras hanging around their necks. They were all staring at our car.

"Who are they?" I asked Nick.

"That's the paparazzi," he said. "They hang around on the look-out for famous people. They take photographs and sell them to the newspapers."

Declan appeared through the front door of the gallery. Nick got out and opened Dad's door, then came round to the side and pulled the door open for Mum.

"Welcome, everyone!" said Declan, shaking hands with Mum as she got out of the car. Mabel went all shy and hid her face in Mum's neck.

I took a deep breath and climbed out as well. All of a sudden there was an explosion of flashes. At first, I thought something terrible was happening, but then I saw that it was the paparazzi people with the cameras. They strained against the rope and a security guard put out his arm to stop them going any further. They were all shouting. At *me*.

"Cole! Over here!"

"This way, Cole! Look at the camera! Look at me!"

"Cole! How does it feel to be a world-famous artist?"

I blinked as the flashes dazzled my eyes. I couldn't see a thing. Why were they taking my picture? I wasn't famous! Declan herded us towards the entrance.

"Come on, let's get you inside," he said, ushering us into the reception. My heart was pounding and my ears were ringing.

"What just happened?" asked Mum breathlessly. Mabel peeked out from Mum's shoulder, her bottom lip sticking out. Declan laughed.

"They just want a photo of Cole, that's all. The fact that we haven't revealed your painting yet is driving everyone *crazy*."

He turned to me.

"Don't be surprised if your photo is on the front pages of *all* the papers tomorrow. And I mean *all* of them. This is worldwide news! *Everyone* wants to know about the art world's newest star, Cole Miller!"

He grinned but I didn't smile back. I glanced at Mason and Mum and Dad. They all looked as shocked as I felt.

"Guys, don't look so worried! I can imagine it's a

bit strange, having all of this attention, but I'm sure you'll get used to it," said Declan. "Right, let's get you mingling, shall we? Marika is very keen to meet you both, Mr and Mrs Miller. And, Cole, there are *a lot* of people who want to talk to you. Follow me!"

Mum put Mabel down on the floor and my little sister gripped her hand tightly. Dad put his hand on the small of Mum's back and Mason walked beside me. I was about to ask Declan where the nearest toilet was when we entered a large white room. It was full of people with shiny hair and expensive-looking clothes, drinking from long, sparkly glasses. Every single one turned around and the room went silent.

"Ladies and gentleman," called Declan. "It gives me great pleasure to introduce to you Marika Loft's incredible protégé ... Cole Miller!"

"What's a protégé?" whispered Mason.

"I have no idea," I whispered back.

Declan quickly swept him, Mum, Dad and Mabel to one side while I stood on my own in front of everyone.

The crowd grinned and awkwardly clapped their hands together while trying to hold on to their glasses of champagne. I tried to smile but it felt more like a grimace and I could feel my face begin to burn.

I recognized at least three actors, a rapper who had been number one last year, and a woman who presented a game show on TV. Once the applause died down some of the crowd came towards me, their teeth dazzling white.

"Cole! How marvellous to meet you," said a lady in a long, blue dress. "Are you looking forward to this evening?"

I smiled back at her. "I guess so," I said.

She looked around her and then leant in towards me, using her hand to shield her mouth.

"Tell me … do you have a whole pile of paintings in your studio, ready to be sold? I'd be very interested in buying them, you know… Very interested indeed."

"Um. I don't have a studio," I said in my best posh voice. "I keep them under my bed."

The lady in the blue dress blinked at me for a moment and then threw her head back and began to laugh.

"Oh, Jeremy!" she said to a large man standing behind her. "He's such a *darling*!"

My family and Mason pushed their way back to join me.

"You OK, champ?" said Dad, whispering in my

ear. I nodded. The lady in blue turned to Mum and I heard her asking where we lived and then the large man turned to Dad.

"I'm Jeremy Dickenson!" he bellowed. He was wearing a white suit and a black shirt that was nearly bursting open over his stomach.

"Pleased to meet you," said Dad, shaking his hand. "I'm Doug. Doug Miller."

"Good to see you, Doug!" shouted Jeremy. "What an incredibly thrilling evening for you all!"

He didn't seem able to talk at a normal volume. I expect he spent a lot of time at loud parties.

"Yes, we're all really excited, aren't we, Cole?" Mabel appeared by Dad's side and tugged on his arm and he picked her up on to his hip.

"So, what is it that you do, Doug?" said Jeremy, looking at Dad inquisitively.

"Do?" said Dad. Mabel started tugging on Dad's earlobes. She pulled one, then reached around his face for the other.

"Stop it, Mabel," he said quietly.

I looked up at my dad as he took Mabel's hand off his ear.

"Ah!" said Dad. "Well, as you can see, I've got my hands full with this little one."

Jeremy paused for a moment, then erupted into possibly one of the loudest laughs I've ever heard.

"No, old chap!" he said. "I don't mean right now! I mean what is your job? Your employment? Are you in the city? Are you in finance?"

Mabel had stopped pulling Dad's ears and was staring at the man. Dad moved her over on to his other hip.

"At the moment I'm a full-time parent," said Dad. "My wife Jenny works and I . . . well, I look after the kids."

Jeremy blinked at Dad. He paused for a moment.

"Why?" he said.

"Well, I'm sure you know what childcare costs can be like," said Dad, smiling. "Until I can find a job that fits around the children we just decided that it would be better if—"

But Jeremy had apparently spotted somebody he knew in the crowd.

"BIANCA!" he bellowed, completely ignoring the fact that Dad was halfway through a sentence and marching off to the other side of the room. As he disappeared into the crowd, it slowly parted and there was a hushed silence as someone made their way through. It was Marika Loft. She was wearing similar clothes to the ones she'd worn to our school – wide-legged trousers, high heels and a shirt – but this time her outfit was grey. Painting 'A Sky in Blue' felt like a lifetime ago now. I watched as she said hello to Mum and Dad, shaking their hands and giving them the biggest, warmest smile. Then she came towards me.

"How are you, Cole?" she said, putting her arm in mine.

"Um. I'm OK," I croaked. I looked around me but my family and Mason had already been swept away into the crowd.

"You should be very proud," she said. "It is an incredible piece of work. It tells such a *story*."

I nodded. My throat felt really dry, and when I swallowed it hurt. A man appeared in front of us. It was Declan.

"Can I just interrupt you there for a moment please, Marika," he said. "We want to get a photograph of Cole next to the cloaked painting before the big reveal."

"Cloaked?" I said.

"The painting is covered with a sheet," said Marika, her violet eyes twinkling. "We're going to unveil it just as the auction begins!"

My heart raced. I looked around the room at all these people, waiting to buy *my* picture.

"Actually, I am a bit worried about the painting," I blurted out. "I'm ... I'm not sure you should sell it. I, I don't think it's my best work."

Marika and Declan both blinked at me. Then Marika began to laugh.

"But of course we're selling it!" she said. She dropped her voice. "Don't worry, Cole. There are *plenty* of wealthy people in this room who are prepared to spend *a lot* of money to get their hands on some of your early work. Have confidence: you're a once-in-a-generation talent."

I opened my mouth to say that I wasn't, but Declan took my arm and began to guide me to the front of the room. As we walked through the crowd, I could hear people discussing me in excited whispers.

"Oh look, Yvette. That's him!"

"He's so little! Is he really twelve years old?"

"Isn't it amazing how someone so young can have so much talent?"

"I hear his family are terribly poor. What an incredible rags-to-riches story."

"Yes, the dad's unemployed and the mother is soon to be out of a job."

I kept my head down as Declan batted them away with his charming grin.

We came to a small stage lit with spotlights. On the plain white wall was my painting, covered with a black sheet. A photographer appeared and immediately began to give me orders.

"Stand on the left of the painting, twist your body towards me, and keep your hands in your pockets," she barked. I walked to the wall, took a deep breath and then turned to face the photographer. I scanned the room for my family. I could just see the top of Mum's head but she wasn't looking in my direction.

"Hands in pockets," said the photographer. "Twist a little more to the side . . . a bit more . . . a bit more. . ."

I turned awkwardly and she moved around me, taking hundreds of photos. She stepped closer, then back a bit, and then she got me to look over my shoulder towards her. The flash from the camera was making my eyes water and I quickly wiped them with my sleeve.

I blinked against the flashes and suddenly Mum was there, right behind the photographer, looking concerned. Declan spotted her and clapped his hands together.

"Right. I think you've got the shot," he said. "Come

on, Cole. We'll get you over to Marika. The time has come for the big reveal!"

The bright spotlights and the flashes had made me feel dizzy. Someone put a glass of water in front of me and I took it and had a big gulp. It was Mason.

"Are you all right?" he asked. I shook my head.

"I want to go home," I told him, but it was too late. The auction was about to start.

CHAPTER TWENTY-FOUR

The Big Reveal

I stood beside the painting and looked out at the crowd. Mum and Dad were standing right at the front, looking up at me with proud smiles on their faces, while Mabel skidded around them in her new silver shoes.

Someone tapped the side of a champagne glass and everybody hushed as a woman stepped up to a lectern and switched on a microphone.

"That's the auctioneer," whispered Marika, appearing next to me. "She's one of the best in the country."

"Ladies and gentlemen, can I have your attention please?" said the woman. "If you are intending to join in with the auction then can I please ask you to refer to your buyer's guide for the terms and conditions of this sale *before* you place your bid."

She held up a little booklet. It had a photograph of the painting, covered with the black cloth on the front. A few people in the crowd fumbled with their guides as the auctioneer continued.

"Before we reveal this wonderful work of art and begin the bidding process, I'd like to pass the microphone over to the person who has made this quite remarkable event happen, Marika Loft."

Everyone applauded as Marika walked to the lectern.

"Thank you," she said into the microphone. "And welcome to my gallery. As you know, we have a rather remarkable young person in the room this evening."

I skimmed my eyes around the crowd as I wasn't really sure where to look. Rows of teeth grinned back at me. I turned to listen to Marika and tried to smile.

"This young man has the kind of talent that only comes along once in a generation, and we are so incredibly lucky to be witnessing the start of his artistic career, right here and right now."

There was another smattering of applause.

"But before we begin, I'd like to ask Cole about his

inspiration for the painting that we are going to be auctioning here tonight."

I gulped nervously. She hadn't told me I would need to speak! I caught Mum's eye and she nodded, encouragingly.

"Cole. We're all *dying* to hear from you. Can you first of all reveal the title of your new masterpiece?"

I looked out at the audience, blinking at the bright lights. And then I leant towards the microphone.

"It's called 'Catch'," I said, my voice wobbling.

There was an "Oohhhh" from the crowd and another ripple of applause. I looked towards Mum, who had Mabel in her arms.

"And, Cole," continued Marika, "can you share with us your inspiration behind 'Catch'?"

I paused for a moment, trying to think of what I should say, what all of these arty people would expect me to tell them.

"So, 'Catch' is about... It's about family and um..." I spotted Mason who was grinning at me. "... friendship."

Marika nodded enthusiastically.

"And the title, Cole: 'Catch'. Would you like to explain what the title means?"

"I guess ... it's like ... the game," I said slowly.

She nodded. "You need two people to play catch, just like you, um, need your friends and family in this . . . ummm . . . crazy game of . . . life."

A big "Ahhhh" came from the crowd and they started clapping.

I exhaled. What a load of nonsense, but it seemed to have gone well. Marika and I stood next to the painting. The auctioneer returned to the microphone.

"Well, I'm sure that you are all *longing* to see 'Catch' for yourselves, and to start the bidding of course!" said the auctioneer. "Cole? Would you like to reveal your painting after a count of three?"

I stepped closer to the wall and held on to the corner of the black fabric.

This was it.

I was going to show the whole world the painting, and if it went well, all of our money worries would be solved.

I looked up as a sea of glowing mobile phones pointed towards me. The official photographer was at the front of the crowd, her camera ready to capture this moment for ever.

"Ladies and gentlemen, can we have a countdown?" asked the auctioneer.

"Three, two, one!" called the crowd. I pulled

the cloth and 'Catch' by Cole Miller was there for everyone to see.

There was a huge gasp, and then silence.

I squeezed my eyes together. I couldn't bear to look. They hated it! That was it. It was all over. I'd utterly failed.

I took a deep breath, bracing myself for everyone to start laughing, but suddenly there was thunderous applause. I opened my eyes and blinked. Everyone was grinning at me! I felt my lips curl up and I grinned back. I searched again for my family. Mum was jiggling around with Mabel, a huge smile on her face, and Dad was pounding his hands together. He gave me a little wave and I waved back.

Then I spotted Mason. He was standing next to Dad, his jaw dangling open as he stared at the painting. He looked at me, at the painting, and then at me again. Our eyes locked. His gaping mouth slowly closed and I read his lips across the crowd.

"What. Have. You. Done?" he said, shaking his head.

CHAPTER TWENTY-FIVE

The Auction

The applause was so loud I could feel it thundering inside my ribcage. As soon as it began to die down, the auctioneer started to speak.

"So, there we have it, everybody," she said. "'Catch' by Cole Miller. Set to be one of the most celebrated early works of our time. Now, who wants to start the bidding at ten thousand pounds? I have ten thousand, can I see eleven?"

What?! Ten thousand pounds already? I stared at a man who was waving his pamphlet in the air.

"Eleven thousand to the gentleman . . . do we have twelve?"

I looked over at Dad as the money kept climbing.

He gave me a thumbs-up, his eyes wide. Mason had his arms folded.

"... so that's seventeen thousand; do I see eighteen?"

Eighteen thousand?! The bidding was going up really, really fast. I was getting hot under the spotlights and I edged to one side to get out of the glare. I saw Mabel in Mum's arms; she was trying to say something, but Mum was shaking her head. Mabel was having none of it.

"Do I see twenty-six thousand anywhere?" continued the auctioneer. "Twenty-six thousand for this wonderful—"

"Forty thousand!" shouted a man at the back.

A few people laughed and cheered. The auctioneer looked shocked. I don't think it was supposed to work like that.

"OK. Well, if you want to jump ahead with a higher bid, sir, then do be my guest. Ladies and gentlemen, we are now at forty thousand for this wonderful painting 'Catch', by Cole Miller. Do I see forty-five? I must say, this is an incredible sum..."

I couldn't believe it! Forty-five thousand? This was life-changing! As the price went up, I kept an eye on Mum and Mabel. Mabel had her arm stretched out, pointing towards the painting behind me on the wall. Her face was bright red and streaked with tears and snot.

"I have fifty thousand. Do I have fifty-five? Fifty-five thousand, thank you. Sixty thousand. Sixty-five thousand. Seventy thousand."

Across the crowd hands shot up as people bid. I spotted Jeremy, the large man who had been rude to Dad, waving his pamphlet, but he stopped at sixty thousand. In the corner was a man on a computer who was taking bids via the internet, and beside him were three people on the phone, bidding on behalf of people at the other end of the line. It was hectic and loud and fast and absolutely *incredible*.

"… we are at seventy thousand pounds, ladies and gentlemen. Seventy thousand pounds. Do I see seventy-five?"

I felt shaky. The bidding was going up and up but I wanted it to stop. This was all too much. Marika looked over at me, her hands pressed together at her lips. I looked away and tried to find Mum again; she was jiggling Mabel up and down on her hip, but Mabel was sobbing. She held on to Mum's face with both hands and as she cried she shouted something at her. I saw the whites of Mum's eyes as she began to get really angry. She snapped something back and my little sister's face crumpled and she dropped her forehead on to Mum's shoulder.

"Ninety thousand pounds! Well, this is incredible, I must say," said the auctioneer. "Did you ever dream that your work would be in such huge demand, Cole?" I shook my head, unable to speak. The audience laughed.

"Do I have ninety-five thousand?"

There were fewer people bidding now. It appeared to be down to someone on the internet, a man at the very back, and a lady who was holding two glasses of champagne and appeared to be a bit unsteady on her feet. The man on the computer who was monitoring the online bids raised his hand.

"Ninety-five!" he called. The audience gasped.

"Ninety-five thousand pounds! My goodness," said the auctioneer.

I couldn't believe it. We could get a car! A holiday! The whole house decorated!

"Do I have one hundred thousand pounds? Madam?" The lady at the front with the drinks shook her head, but then the man at the back suddenly shot his hand up into the air and waved his leaflet.

"ONE HUNDRED THOUSAND POUNDS to

the gentleman at the back of the room!" cried the auctioneer.

"That's one hundred thousand pounds, ladies and gentlemen. One hundred thousand. Do we have one hundred and ten?" She looked around the room. The man on the computer turned around and shook his head.

"One hundred thousand, then. Are we all done? Going once, going twice, and SOLD to you, sir, for one hundred thousand pounds!"

BANG!

The auctioneer slammed the wooden gavel on to the lectern.

That was it. It was all over. The room erupted into cheers and whoops. People crowded around me and I felt hundreds of hands patting me on the back.

"Well done!" said Marika, holding me by my shoulders. "It's an incredible piece of work. *Incredible.*"

"That was amazing!" said Declan, giving me a squeeze on the arm. "My phone is going crazy already. Everyone wants you! The TV news team want to do a live interview from your house next week. Isn't that great?"

Live TV? I still couldn't speak. My legs felt like

jelly and I was trying hard to keep upright. Was this actually happening? My ears were still ringing from the sound of the wooden hammer banging down as the painting sold. The crowd around me began to chatter about how it had been the most exciting auction they'd ever seen. And then, for the first time that evening, I turned to take a proper look at the painting behind me.

The painting I'd titled 'Catch'. But this wasn't my picture of a wonky chair and a tennis ball.

On this canvas were two rectangular shapes, one red and one grey. The shapes both had a triangle beside them, and dots had been speckled all around. Dots made by fingertips much smaller than mine. In the bottom left-hand corner was a dark-blue, curly C. A signature that said that this piece of artwork had been created by me. Cole Miller.

But it hadn't.

It had been painted by my three-year-old sister in my bedroom just days ago. The one of me and her playing the butterfly game.

And someone had just bought it for one hundred thousand pounds.

CHAPTER TWENTY-SIX

Going Home

I pressed my forehead against the cold car window. It was dark and drizzling in London, but there were still plenty of people scurrying around the streets as we passed by. Dad was in the front of the car, talking to Nick, the driver. He kept saying, "I can't believe it. All that money!" over and over again. I think he was in shock.

Mum was scrolling through her phone. She turned around.

"Cole! You're all over Twitter and Instagram!"

I smiled but my face dropped when she turned back.

Mabel was asleep, her head resting on the side of

the car seat as she breathed gently. Her cheeks were red and blotchy from all of her crying earlier. By the time I saw my family after the auction had finished, Mabel had calmed down and was more interested in eating a pastry than saying anything about her painting causing all that fuss. Mum and Dad had thrown their arms around me as I looked at Mason over their shoulders. He just shook his head.

"The first thing we'll do is get the whole house decorated," said Mum, turning around again. "Does that sound OK, Cole? And Mabel desperately needs some new clothes; she's growing out of hers so fast. And maybe we could even look at taking a holiday. Wouldn't that be great? I can't remember the last time we all went away."

"That'll be nice," I said quietly. She turned back to her phone. Mason thumped me on the arm.

"I saw your painting and the one they just sold was definitely *not* yours," he hissed. "That was Mabel's painting!"

"Shhhhh. Keep your voice down," I said. He leant closer to me.

"It's fraud!" said Mason. "Whoever bought that painting believed it was by you and it's not. It was bad enough to pay a ton of money for something *you've*

216

done, but now they've ended up with one by a three-year-old! Can you imagine how much trouble you're going to be in when they find out?"

Mason looked really worried and it made me feel even more sick.

"I panicked!" I said. "And anyway, it was YOU who put the idea into my head by saying Mabel's picture was better than mine! I sent a photo to Declan and I didn't think they'd like it, but they did!'

He was about to say something else when Nick called out from the front of the car. "Listen up, everyone!" He turned the volume up on the radio.

"There was huge excitement this evening at the Marika Loft Gallery when twelve-year-old artist Cole Miller sold a painting for one hundred thousand pounds. The auction has attracted worldwide attention and has provoked a question amongst critics and the public alike – what makes something a piece of art? Marika Loft spoke after the auction, defending the artist's young age and stressing that important works can be produced by anybody. The painting sold to an anonymous bidder, believed to be a private collector."

Dad gave a little clap as Nick turned the radio down.

"Did you hear that, Cole?" whispered Mason,

his eyes growing bigger. "Worldwide attention. *Worldwide*. It isn't just the people in the gallery that you've lied to. Or the man who bought the picture. Or your mum and dad. Or Mabel. It's *everyone*."

We stared at each other and I took a deep breath. He was right.

Somehow, I'd just managed to fool the entire world.

CHAPTER TWENTY-SEVEN

Shopping Spree

I woke the next day to the sound of Mum shouting from the lounge.

"COLE! YOU'RE ON THE TELLY!"

I jumped out of bed and ran downstairs. Mum was on her knees in front of the TV and Dad was leaning forward in the armchair. There was a picture of 'Catch' next to a photo of me.

"*...the identity of the bidder has not been confirmed, but what we do know is that it sold for an extraordinary sum for a new artist. One hundred thousand pounds. The story has been receiving attention from around the world...*"

"Amazing," said Dad. He was still in a daze.

Mabel suddenly scooted into the lounge and I quickly scooped her up before she could see her painting on the TV.

"Shall we go and find some breakfast, Mabel?" I said. She stared at me, a bit bewildered. I wasn't usually this happy to see her.

I trotted to the kitchen and put Mabel on the floor. All the fuss would die down soon; I just needed to get through the next couple of days without her being reminded of the painting and giving the game away. Mum came into the kitchen.

"Declan said we should have the money in our account by Wednesday – isn't that great?"

I tipped some cereal into a bowl and Mabel opened the drawer and helped herself to a yellow plastic spoon.

"Me and your dad were thinking we could all go to the retail park today and look for a new sofa."

"I don't have to come, do I?" I said, putting some cereal into a bowl for myself.

"You don't have to, but I'd like you to," said Mum. That was her way of telling me I had to. "Oh, and Declan messaged me this morning asking about your next painting. Did he text you too?"

"I haven't looked at my phone yet," I lied.

I'd seen the text as soon as I'd woken up. He'd asked if I could get my next painting finished as soon as possible as he had a waiting list of buyers. The text had made me feel sick so I deleted it without replying.

"So, how does it feel to be famous, son?" said Dad, coming into the kitchen and flicking the switch on the kettle.

I shrugged and shoved a great spoonful of cereal into my mouth. The dry, sharp edges scratched at my throat and it hurt as I tried to swallow them down.

"Jenny, I was thinking we could take the kids for lunch at that new bistro on the edge of the retail park. How about it?"

I looked at Mum. I couldn't remember us ever going out for lunch before.

Mum frowned. "It's a bit expensive in there, isn't it?" she said.

"But we've got some money left over from the first painting and more to come. I think we're allowed a little celebration, don't you, Mabel?"

Mabel waved her spoon in the air when she heard her name, shooting cereal pieces everywhere. Mum and Dad laughed.

*

The bus to the retail park was busy, and me and Dad had to stand for most of the journey. I really wasn't in the mood to be dragged around a furniture shop and thought about asking if I could wait outside, but I knew Mum wouldn't let me.

We headed straight to Furniture Unlimited and Mum and Dad kept giggling and oohing and ahhing over boring things like lamps and cushions. We got to the sofa section and Mum ran around practically squealing. It was so embarrassing.

"Look at this one, Doug! It reclines!" said Mum. She sat on a grey sofa and pulled a handle down by her side, and her legs shot up into the air. Dad laughed and tried the armchair. Mabel had discovered a swivel chair beside a desk and was busy spinning herself round and round. I stood next to her and pretended that the two grown adults getting excited about soft furnishings didn't belong to me.

"Come and try it, Cole! It's so much more comfortable than our old one," called Mum, patting the seat beside her.

Mabel and I sat down next to her. I sank backwards against the cushions. The material was soft and the sofa didn't sink in the middle like the one at home.

"What do you think, Cole?" said Dad. "Do you think it'll look nice in our lounge? We'll probably get the whole house redecorated at some point; we definitely need a new carpet and curtains."

I sat forward.

"It's nice but I don't understand why you're doing all this shopping when you haven't even got the money yet?" I said.

Mum put her hand on my arm.

"It's fine, Cole. We can just pay a deposit for the sofa today and the rest will be due in monthly instalments. You don't need to worry."

Mabel pointed towards some colourful beanbags that were scattered on a big, fluffy rug. She pulled on my hand and we both went over and flopped down on the squishy bags.

Mum and Dad walked around the shop for ages until eventually deciding on the very first sofa, and then they started talking to one of the shop assistants.

"Cole? Can we do more painting soon?" said Mabel. My stomach sank. I ignored her and pretended to pick at something on my jeans

"Cole?" she said again, tapping on my arm. "Mabel likes painting."

I spun around to her.

"No, Mabel. We are not doing any more painting. And if you say *anything* to Mum or Dad about your picture then they are going to be really, really angry with you for touching my paints. OK? They'll probably be so angry they'll throw your butterfly game in the bin!"

Her big eyes blinked at me.

"Butterfly game?" she said, her forehead crinkling.

"Yes! You won't be able to play it ever, ever again."

Mabel's bottom lip curled up over the top and then she screwed up her face and tears began to squeeze out of her eyes, like a tap had been turned on. Mum and Dad appeared.

"What's all this?" said Mum, scooping Mabel into her arms. "Why is she crying, Cole?"

I shrugged.

"I dunno," I said. "I think she needs a nap or something."

"You don't need a nap, do you, Mabel?" said Mum. "You've only just got up."

I climbed out of the beanbag.

"Is there anything you want to look at while we're here, Cole?" said Dad. "There's a sports shop next door. How about we go and check out some trainers?"

My heart leapt. Trainers!

"OK!" I said brightly. Mum said she'd take Mabel to the big toy shop and we arranged to meet at the restaurant for lunch. As we walked, Dad asked me what trainers I might like. He mentioned some brands that were probably fashionable when he was young in the 1990s, but I'd never heard of them.

"I think XT50s are quite nice," I said, remembering Mason's white pair.

We walked into the sports shop and up a big escalator to get to the trainer section. It was really busy. There were cardboard boxes and tissue paper everywhere and I spotted a small boy whose foot was being rammed into a trainer by a man kneeling down in front of him. The two of them were wearing matching black leather jackets.

"Come on, Oakley! Put a bit of effort into it, son. Push!"

The boy didn't appear to be making any attempt to get his white, fluffy-socked toes into the shoe.

"But I don't like 'em, Dad!" said Oakley. "They're 'orrible!"

"Ah, mate. You're killing me, you are," said the dad. He tossed the shoe towards the shop assistant, who caught it with one hand. Oakley picked up his own perfectly new-looking trainer and put it on. His dad muttered under his breath about what a waste of time it had all been and how he was gagging for a Big Mac.

Dad smirked at me, then got the assistant's attention. He was wearing a badge that said his name was Will.

"Excuse me, do you have any XT50s in a size seven for my son?"

Will stared at Dad and then at me.

"Yeah. But they're, like, *really* expensive," he said, looking us both up and down and settling his eyes on my feet. "He can't try them on unless you're serious about buying them. We get a lot of time-wasters."

I felt myself going red. The assistant obviously thought we didn't look like the kind of people who could afford the most expensive trainers in the shop.

"We're serious," said Dad, putting a hand on my shoulder. "Size seven. XT50s."

Will huffed.

"Black or white?" he said to me.

"Black, please," I said. I didn't want to get the same as Mason.

He picked up some of the shoe boxes scattered around the floor and tucked them under his arm.

"Take a seat. I'll check if we've got them in stock," he said. He took a radio out of his back pocket and spoke into it.

"Keiron? Keiron! Wake up!"

There was a crackle as Keiron grunted.

"Mate. We got any XT50s left? Black. Size seven? Not TWs. I repeat, customers are not TWs."

Dad nudged me.

"Did you hear that?" he whispered. "Not TWs. Not time-wasters!" He laughed and I found myself laughing as well. I undid my laces, and then remembered I was wearing some really old socks with holes in the heels.

"Dad? Can I get some socks as well?"

Dad nodded and went over to a revolving stand. He checked the price of a white pair and his eyes widened slightly, before he came back with them. If he thought the socks were expensive, I dreaded to see his reaction to the XT50s.

"Here, put a pair of these on," he said, pulling the white socks from a pack of three. Will stepped forward.

"It's all right," said Dad to him. "We're going to pay for them."

I quickly took off my old socks and put the new pair on. They felt soft and springy underneath. I'd never worn socks like that before: all my pairs were thin and scratchy.

Will's radio crackled again and he went off to a doorway and came back with a shiny black box that he passed to Dad.

"These are the last pair in stock. Even if they don't fit you can probably sell them for more money on eBay or something…" There was a crash as someone knocked a load of toddler trainers off a stand and Will went over to sort it out.

Dad opened the box.

"They look … different," he said. I peered in and saw the black trainers nestled in white tissue paper. They didn't look different, they looked *incredible*. I picked one up and studied it closely. It was so light! The large plastic soles had a transparent part near the heel. Inside you could see three silver spheres which squished down when you walked. I quickly put my foot into the shoe and stood up. It felt like I was standing on a cloud.

"Oh wow, they're so comfortable!" I said, grinning at Dad. He passed me the other shoe and when I put that one on as well it felt like I was actually floating. I walked up and down and then stood in front of a mirror. They looked amazing from the ankle down, but they didn't really go very well with my too-short trousers or scruffy top.

"What do you think, Cole? Are they keepers?" said Dad.

I sat down beside him.

"I don't know," I said. "They're really expensive, Dad." I wanted them but it felt so weird, having something that cost so much money on my feet.

"Cole, if it wasn't for you then we wouldn't be able to get all these things for the house. I think you deserve a treat and if you really want them then you should . . . oh."

Dad looked at the price on the side of the box.

"Excuse me? Will?" he called to the assistant. "I think there's been a mix-up on your pricing here?"

"Sshhh, Dad," I said, between gritted teeth.

"I think a zero has been added on by mistake," he continued.

Will looked at him, blankly, and then began to laugh.

"Ha! Yeah . . . an extra zero! That's funny!" He chuckled to himself then turned back to his customer.

"Dad! That's how much they cost!" I said.

"Crikey, Cole. These cost more than our TV!" said Dad.

I looked at the trainers and then loosened the laces and slipped them off. What on earth was I thinking? Of course we wouldn't be buying them. My family didn't wear shoes that cost three figures. That was money that could probably feed us for the next month. I put the trainers back in the box and covered them with the tissue. It had been nice to try them on, anyway. I put my old shoes on again. They felt hard and heavy.

I took a long breath.

"Don't worry about it, Dad," I said. "I'll just get the socks if that's OK?"

Dad picked up the socks in the ripped packet.

"Right, I'll go and queue up," he said. "I'll meet you downstairs by the door."

I headed to the escalator and stepped on. Around me were hundreds of families carrying shiny, silver bags.

I sighed. It was fine. This world full of expensive labels and walking-on-cloud trainers just wasn't mine. It never had been. We had *far* more important things to spend the money on. Anyway, I didn't have anything nice enough to wear with the XT50s, so what was the point of owning them?

I stepped off the escalator and stood by the door, waiting for Dad.

"Cole! COLE!"

I looked up. Leyton and Niall from school were

coming down the escalator towards me. I gave them both a weak smile. Just my luck.

"Dad said you were on the news today!" shouted Leyton, jumping off the moving stair and coming over. "You here to spend your money, are you, Poor Kid Cole? Getting some decent gear at last?"

They laughed and I laughed back.

"Yeah, something like that," I said, trying to sound like I wasn't bothered by his comment.

"At least your dad won't ever need to get a job now, eh?" jeered Niall. "He can just stay on the dole for ever!" I thought about saying, for the thousandth time, that Dad wasn't actually on the dole, he was a stay-at-home father, when I saw him getting off the escalator behind them.

"Here you go, son," he said, passing me a silver bag. I looked at the bag. Inside were the white socks, and a shiny black shoebox.

"You got them?!" I said. "You actually got them?"

"Of course I did!" said Dad, then turned to Leyton and Niall. "Oh, hello. Are you friends of Cole's?"

They nodded silently, their eyes fixed on the shoebox as I took it out of the bag. I opened it up.

"Whoa ... are they XT50s?" said Niall, unable to keep the astonishment out of his voice.

I nodded.

"Can I wear them now?" I asked.

"'Course you can," said Dad.

I quickly took off my shoes and stuffed them into the carrier bag and put the trainers on. They made me nearly three inches taller.

"They are *sooo* cool," said Leyton, his voice trembling.

"They're the last pair they had," I said, twisting my feet this way and that. "They are *so* comfortable."

"My mum would *never* buy me shoes that expensive," said Niall. "You are *so* lucky."

I grinned at them both.

"Come on then, Cole," said Dad. "If we're quick we can get you some new clothes before we have lunch."

"I'd better get going," I said, as if I was annoyed that I couldn't stay and chat to them for longer. "See you tomorrow!"

I walked away as Leyton and Niall stood with their jaws hanging open, their eyes fixed on my brand-new trainers.

Being rich was going to be a lot of fun.

CHAPTER TWENTY-EIGHT

Live TV

The next day there was a crowd of people waiting for me in the playground.

"Have you brought your XT50s in? Can I see them?"

"My dad reckons your next painting might sell for half a million! Do you think it will?"

"Cole! Is it true you're getting a Ferrari?"

I looked around at everyone and grinned.

"I can't comment, I'm afraid," I said, smiling. "Maybe."

Niall slung his arm around my shoulders.

"Do you fancy coming round mine later? Mum said she'd do us some burgers."

I shook my head.

"I can't. I've got a TV crew coming round tonight," I said, sniffing. "They want to do a live interview with me."

A few people gasped.

"Are you going on the telly?!" said Kiki. "What time?"

"During the five o'clock news, I think," I said. "I'll have to ask Declan. I mean, Marika's PA."

"Hey, Cole. Do you wanna come go-karting on Saturday?" asked Leyton.

Niall took his arm off my shoulders and scowled at Leyton as they both waited to hear what I'd say.

"Sure," I said casually. "Sounds good." Leyton fist-punched the air and I carried on walking through the crowd. I spotted Mason and Isla sitting on a bench, watching, and I went over to join them.

"You all right?" I said.

"Yep," said Mason. "What was that about?" I turned around and everyone was still staring at me.

"Oh, you know. Everyone is just a bit overexcited I guess," I said, sitting down. "I'm sure I'll be old news tomorrow!"

Isla smiled but Mason didn't look so happy.

"Now the auction is out of the way we can get back

to solving 'An Enigma in Oil'," said Isla. "You know the clue about listening to the river? Well, I think it means that..."

I held my hand up to stop her.

"I'm sorry, Isla, but I don't really need to solve the riddle any more," I said.

"What?" said Isla. "But we've come so far!"

I saw Mason check the time on his watch. I made a mental note to have a look at some new watches for myself when I got the chance. Maybe a smart watch so it was different to his. *Better* than his.

"There probably isn't any treasure anyway. It's probably just a big joke. Besides, I'm too busy now, what with all the press and interest in my art," I said.

The bell went for registration and Mason and Isla stood up and walked off. As I followed they whispered something to each other and Mason shook his head. I guessed they were talking about me. I felt like somehow I was letting them down. But I just didn't have time to run around a museum looking for treasure that probably didn't exist. What was the point in that?

When I got home from school there was a huge TV truck parked outside our house. A few of our neighbours were standing out on the street, pointing and chatting to each other. I waved at them, then went indoors.

Cables came out of the truck, along our path and hallway and snaked into our lounge. I could hear Dad talking to the engineers about his old job as a music roadie.

"Hi, Cole," said a young woman, coming out of our kitchen and holding a cup of tea. "I'm Tasmin and I'll be doing your interview today. Congratulations on your big sale! You must be incredibly excited."

"Hi," I said. "Yes, it's been amazing."

She was wearing a lot of make-up and her eyelashes were so long they touched her eyebrows.

"I've just been explaining to your parents how this is going to work. We'd like to have the four of you sitting on the sofa, with you in the middle and then—"

"The four of us?" I interrupted. The woman nodded. "Yes. You, your mum and dad and your little sister is going to sit on your mum's lap."

"Mabel?" I said. "Why does she have to be there?"

"Our viewers will want to see all of you!" said Tasmin brightly. "We're going to link up with Romesh in the studio just after five-fifteen. I'll ask you a few questions and you just answer them as best you can."

"OK," I said. Tasmin went into the lounge and I headed to the kitchen.

Mum was at the table with Mabel sat beside her who was scribbling her crayons over a picture of a zebra in her new colouring book. She hadn't mentioned her painting since I got angry with her in the furniture shop. With any luck, she'd forgotten all about it.

"Are you all right, Cole?" said Mum.

"Yep!" I said brightly. Although I was suddenly feeling incredibly nervous. "I'll just go and get changed." I ran upstairs and put on a pair of jeans and a soft hoodie that I'd bought at the retail park yesterday. I slipped my feet into my new XT50s and took a look in my mirror. I swallowed. Was that really me? Wearing designer clothes and looking ... wealthy? I smiled at my reflection, but my mouth didn't look quite right. I shrugged, then headed back downstairs to the kitchen.

"Your dad is getting Mabel changed," said Mum, sipping at her tea. She was quiet for a moment and then she looked up.

"It's quite overwhelming, isn't it? All this attention," she said. She got up from the table and closed the kitchen door, then sat back down, her hands curled around the cup. "Don't get me wrong, it's really exciting and a wonderful thing to happen to us, but ... it feels ... it feels a bit like we're trapped in one of those snow globes. And that we've been shaken and everyone is looking in on us."

I nodded. I knew exactly what she meant. The kitchen door opened and a head popped around the side.

"Are we all good to go?"

It was Tasmin. Mum got up.

"Ready?" she said to me with a smile. I smiled back.

"Ready," I said.

The lounge was jammed full of people and equipment. Our TV was on in the corner, the sound muted. It looked like the news presenters were talking about the sport and they were showing the clip of a goal in a football match.

"If you want to sit there, Mrs Miller, that's great," said Tasmin. "And if you go in the middle, Cole." I sat down. Dad appeared with Mabel. She stretched her arms towards Mum and Dad put her on her lap.

"Mr Miller, if you could sit on the end ... and that's great!" said Tasmin. It was a bit of a squash.

"It's a shame we haven't got our new sofa yet, eh, Cole?" said Dad, patting the arm of the chair and releasing another cloud of dust. Fortunately, nobody seemed to notice.

"Right," said Tasmin, checking her notes. "I'm going to start with a brief hello to Romesh in the studio, and then I'll turn to you guys and we can have a chat. It's all very relaxed, nothing to worry about."

"Can we keep the TV on?" said Dad. "It's nice to see what's going on in the studio."

The sports news had moved on to rugby now and they were showing a clip of Wales scoring a try. Tasmin thought about it for a moment.

"OK... But we'll need to keep it muted. And please, please, don't stare at it when we're doing the interview."

She flicked through her notes.

"When I talk to Romesh I can hear what he's saying through my earpiece but you won't be able to, OK?" She flashed her teeth at us and stared at her notes again. I noticed Mum was gripping on to Mabel. She looked utterly terrified. Tasmin pressed the earpiece into her ear. "They are just going to recap the news headlines and then it's us. Get ready, team."

On our TV I could see a different presenter at a desk, reading the headlines. The news went by in a flash and before we knew it we were live to the whole country. I glanced at our TV again and saw Romesh, the presenter, with us sitting on our sofa on a big screen behind him. I quickly looked at Tasmin. She was staring straight down the lens of the camera.

"Yes, hi, Romesh! I'm here this evening with the Miller family. They had rather an exciting evening on Saturday at a prestigious art gallery in London. Cole, would you like to tell me what happened?"

She pointed the black microphone towards my face. My instinct was to hold it but she moved it out of my reach.

"I ... I sold a painting," I said. I glanced at the TV behind her and saw that the whole country was now seeing the four of us in close up. It was surreal. Tasmin turned to the camera and laughed.

"But this wasn't just any painting, Romesh; this was a painting discovered by one of the most iconic artists our country has ever known: Marika Loft. Would you like to tell us how much the painting went for, Cole?"

I looked beyond the microphone and saw a photograph of Mabel's painting on the screen. I swallowed.

"It sold for one hundred thousand pounds."

"That's a remarkable sum of money, isn't it?" she said. "For *any* artist, but especially one of your age!" I nodded. She hovered the microphone in front of me for a while, but I couldn't get any more words out.

"So, Jenny," she said, moving on to Mum. "How does it feel to have such a talented son?"

"It has been very exciting," said Mum quietly. Tasmin moved the microphone a little closer. "But he'll always be just Cole to us."

Tasmin grinned.

"Our Cole but with more expensive footwear!" laughed Dad. Tasmin laughed too.

"I see! So, you've already been spending some of the money, have you, Cole? What else are you planning on buying?"

I opened my mouth but nothing came out. Dad leant forwards.

"We've had quite a few tough years financially. Cole has kindly agreed that we should spend some of the money on essentials for the home. As well as the trainers, of course!"

"Yes, I understand you've been out of work for a while now, Mr Miller. You were a music roadie, is that right?"

I swallowed. Why was everyone so interested about Dad not having a job?

"I was! For all the big bands. I'm now a full-time father," he said. "Although I am looking for work that fits around the children. You know what childcare costs can be like!"

Tasmin grinned at him, looking a bit blank. I was starting to feel really uncomfortable, when Mabel suddenly sat up from Mum's lap. She pointed her hand towards our TV.

"Look!" she shouted.

On our TV was what everybody around the country was seeing. A photograph of 'Catch' on the wall in the gallery.

Tasmin laughed.

"I think the viewers at home can now see Cole's painting that sold for the incredible sum of one hundred thousand pounds," said Tasmin.

"MY painting!" Mabel said at the top of her voice. The TV cut back to us on the sofa.

"Ah, that's so sweet!" said Tasmin, turning to my little sister. "Did you want to keep Cole's painting for yourself, Mabel?"

"No," said Mabel, shaking her head. "That's Mabel's painting. Cole and Mabel did painting! I got my hands *all* messy!" She wiggled her fingers towards Tasmin.

"Not this again, Mabel," said Mum. "That's *Cole's* picture. We went to the auction where it sold for lots of money. Remember?"

Mabel shook her head.

"IT'S MABEL'S!" she said at the top of her lungs. "Mabel did 'dot' 'dot' 'dot' with her fingers and her hand went SPLODGE!"

Mabel looked at me and grinned. I scowled back.

"And then Cole hid Mabel's painting under his bed!" she said, wriggling on Mum's lap. She pulled the microphone really close to her lips. "Sssshhhh," she said, into the black foam mic. "It's a *secret*."

I froze and stared down at my knees as Mabel squirmed in Mum's arms.

"Cole?" whispered Dad on my other side. "What's going on?" I didn't look at anyone. If I stayed completely still and didn't make eye contact then perhaps Tasmin would move the conversation on. My heart sank as she pressed her ear, listening to something through her earpiece.

"Yes, Romesh. This does indeed appear to be a very interesting development happening *live* here in the Miller household," said Tasmin, her eyes twinkling.

The TV screen had changed back to the painting 'Catch', but this time they had zoomed in on the little dots that made up the butterflies around the oblong shapes. The ones made by Mabel's tiny fingers.

"I believe the viewers at home can now see a close-up of your painting, Cole. And yes, I can see that those little dots appear to be made by some particularly small fingertips. Possibly ones smaller than your own?"

The camera moved around and then focused in on the tiny portion of handprint that Mabel had accidentally put in one corner.

"And I think we can see ... yes, we can see a handprint right there! An incredibly small handprint ... like a toddler's..."

Mabel clapped as she saw the close-up on our TV.

"Mabel's hand!" she squealed. "Mabel's hand went SPLODGE and I got all messy! That's Mabel's painting!"

I knew that everyone was staring at me, waiting for me to say something, but I stayed silent.

"Cole? Mr and Mrs Miller? I'm sure our audience at home would be very interested to hear your comments about this."

The black microphone pointed at Mum and then Dad. Both of them had their jaws dangling open.

In my head it felt like our house was collapsing around us. A scene of absolute devastation. The walls slowly crumbled as a cloud of dust and debris circled the lounge. All that remained was a TV camera, a reporter and a family of four, squashed together on a scruffy sofa.

I stared at the microphone and then I glanced up at Tasmin. She looked utterly delighted.

"Come on, Cole," she said. "Those tiny fingerprints and that handprint weren't made by you. Were they? In fact, it looks like this painting isn't yours at all, is it?"

I stared towards the ground and focused on a thinning patch of carpet. Maybe if I just kept silent they'd give up and cut back to the studio. I waited, but the microphone stayed exactly where it was.

"Cole?" whispered Mum. "What's going on?"

And then Tasmin asked me a question. A question that was about to change everything.

"Cole Miller, the world is waiting. Who actually *is* the artist behind 'Catch'; the painting that has just sold for one hundred thousand pounds?"

I took a deep breath and gulped. I couldn't think of a single thing to say that would get me out of this. The game was up.

"My sister," I whispered.

CHAPTER TWENTY-NINE

The News is Out

Everything that happened next was a blur. Tasmin listened to someone in her earpiece and then she turned to the camera;

"And that's where we'll have to leave it now, but as you can see there are *very* big developments here in the Miller household. Back to Romesh in the studio."

The camera went off and the microphone went down. The cameraman and sound woman immediately began to pack up their things. Tasmin crossed her arms. "Well, it looks like you've got a lot of explaining to do, doesn't it?" she said. "We'll leave you to it."

Mum turned to me as Mabel wriggled off her lap.

My little sister headed to the hallway and I could hear her padding upstairs.

"Cole? What did you mean? Why would you say that Mabel did that painting? It was yours!" Mum's voice was shaking and she was blinking really quickly. I didn't answer.

"Come on, Cole. Why did Mabel say the painting was done by her?" said Dad. "Answer us!"

The TV crew were silently putting away their equipment, but I could tell they were all listening. I stood up and ran upstairs. Mabel was in my room again.

"What did you do that for? You've ruined everything. EVERYTHING," I yelled at her. She frowned at me, then dived on to the floor near my bed. Mum and Dad burst in.

"Cole? What's going on?" said Mum, close to tears.

"Come on, son. You need to explain yourself!" said Dad.

Mabel appeared from beneath my bed with the painting of the chair with the wonky legs and tennis ball on the seat. My painting. The painting that I had also titled 'Catch' in my head.

"Here's Cole's picture!" said Mabel, tapping at it with her finger. She had a big smile on her face. She had no idea how bad this was going to be for me.

"That's Cole's?" said Mum. Mabel nodded.

"Mabel's has gone," she said sadly. "Hammer went BANG!" She thumped her little fist on the floor, just like the auctioneer's gavel. There was no question what she was telling us.

Mum looked a bit sick as she sat down on the bed.

"Was there a mix-up, Cole? Did the wrong painting end up at the gallery?" said Mum.

"Of course!" said Dad, relief washing over his face. "Declan must have taken the wrong one. When we got to the auction you were just too embarrassed to say anything. Isn't that right, Cole?"

I sat on my bed, my legs pulled up and my chin resting on my knees as I stared at my duvet. Mum crouched down beside me.

"This is very serious, darling," she said, putting her hand on my arm. "If this is some kind of misunderstanding then we really need to know so we can explain to everyone that it's just been a big mistake."

My brain was buzzing. I needed more time to think, but they wanted an answer right now. Could I say that somehow the wrong painting was taken that day and I was too worried to say anything when I saw

Mabel's picture on the wall? Like Dad had suggested? I opened my mouth, but the words wouldn't come. I simply couldn't lie any more.

"There was no mix-up," I said firmly. "I pretended Mabel's painting was mine."

Nobody said anything. All you could hear were Mum and Dad's mobile phones vibrating on the kitchen counter downstairs. They sounded like giant wasps trapped in a jam jar. For a second, I wondered if I could just make a run for it. Get away to some place where nobody knew me. But where would I go? Dad shuddered into life.

"Cole? Is that the truth? That you deliberately gave Mabel's painting to Declan and pretended it was yours? And then..." The words caught in his throat. "And then it sold for a hundred thousand pounds?"

I nodded, not meeting his eyes. Mum whimpered and put her hand to her face.

"Do you understand ... do you *actually* understand what you've done?" asked Dad. His eyes looked shimmery like he was about to cry. I'd never seen my dad cry before. And it was all because of me.

"I'm sorry," I whispered.

"You're *sorry*?" he repeated, as if it was the most

stupid thing I'd ever said to him. "Cole, you have made a complete laughing stock of us in front of the WHOLE BLOODY WORLD!"

He shouted so loudly that I flinched and squeezed my eyes shut.

"Doug, calm down," said Mum. I opened my eyes again but Mum looked just as angry as Dad did. Downstairs, their mobile phones stopped ringing for a second, and then started up again. Mabel was silent, looking up at me through her long lashes as she sat on the carpet with my painting.

"I couldn't do it," I said, trying not to cry. "I couldn't do the painting. I tried, Mum, I really did."

Mum nodded as she listened. Dad paced around my room, wringing his hands together.

"I tried so many times. You can ask Mrs Frampton! I went to her classroom every chance I got, but everything I painted just looked awful and Marika didn't like them."

I was hoping that they'd both start to look a bit sympathetic but their faces hadn't changed.

"You should have told us you were struggling," said Dad. "Why didn't you tell us?"

Mum shook her head at him.

"Go on, Cole. Then what happened," she said.

"I was looking after Mabel when Dad went shopping and she started playing with my paints. She squirted some on to a canvas and mixed it around with her fingers."

I looked at Mabel, who stared down at her hands.

"At first, I told her off and said she was making a mess, but then I realized that her picture was far better than anything I had done. I took a photo of it and sent it to Declan. I was expecting them to say it wasn't good enough, but they didn't. They loved it."

I kind of laughed then, hoping they might see a funny side to all of this, but nobody found it amusing.

"And didn't you feel in the slightest bit guilty about what you were doing?" said Dad.

"Yes! But I had to give Marika *something* or she would have cancelled the auction and we wouldn't have made any money. And you and Mum were so excited... I just got carried away, I guess. When Declan came to collect it, I gave him Mabel's picture and pretended it was mine. I even signed it. I had no idea it would sell for that much."

Dad looked livid. "So, you're saying it would have been OK if it had only sold for a thousand pounds? A hundred?" he said.

"Um. Yes?" I said. At least it wouldn't have made the news.

Mum sighed.

"Cole. The painting was a lie, regardless of how much it sold for. Can't you see the wrong in that?"

My throat felt tight as I tried not to cry.

"But that man was so rich he could afford to buy a painting *by a kid* for one hundred thousand pounds! He has far more than we have and we *need* that money. Why does it matter?!"

I saw a tear roll down Mum's face and she quickly brushed it away.

"Because we are better than that, Cole," she said. "We have *never* put money before our integrity. I thought you of all people would understand that."

I sat and blinked at them both.

"Now we know the truth I guess we'll have to go and face everyone. We'll call Marika's office and confirm that the painting isn't yours so they can cancel the sale," said Dad.

I swung my legs around the side of my bed.

"Cancel the sale? B-but the bidder might still want to buy it! It's a good picture. Art is art, that's what Marika says! Anyone can make it!" How could they just give in like this?

Dad rolled his eyes.

"Don't you get it, Cole?" he said. "This isn't us! This family does not tell lies. This family does *not* put money before our moral values."

I glanced at Mum. She looked utterly devastated. She took Mabel's hand and they both left the room.

"What a mess you've got us into, son," Dad said, shaking his head as he followed.

After he'd gone I took a few deep breaths. And then I kicked off my expensive trainers and stuffed them back into their box, throwing them into the corner of my room. I dived on to my bed and lay face down on my pillow.

It was all over. My secret was out and I'd ruined absolutely *everything*. I felt a sob building in the back of my throat but the tears wouldn't come. I'd never seen Mum and Dad look at me like that before: they were so ashamed. I wanted to turn back time to that morning when I took the photograph of Mabel's painting lying on my floor. If only I had pushed hers back under my bed and taken a picture of mine instead. Even if Marika had rejected it and my art career was over before it had really begun, at least I wouldn't have been caught lying to the entire world.

I gulped and let go of the sob, and my shoulders

began to shake as I cried. Before long, my pillow was
soaked with tears.

CHAPTER THIRTY

Cole the Gladiator

When I got to school the next day it became immediately clear that almost everyone had been watching TV last night. I felt like a gladiator entering the ring just at the point the ravenous lions were unleashed. The shouting began as soon as I entered the playground.

"Here he comes! Cheating Cole!"

"CHEAT! CHEAT! CHEAT! CHEAT!"

"Thought you could get away with it, eh, Picasso?"

"I heard his next painting is actually going to be by his DOG!"

Everyone laughed at that one. I was about to point out that I didn't actually own a dog, but then

I remembered that answering back was not a great idea. For anyone who hadn't seen it live on TV, they now had the chance to watch it via YouTube. As I walked through the crowd I could hear Tasmin's voice coming out of hundreds of phones.

"Cole Miller, the world is waiting. Who actually is the artist behind 'Catch'; the painting that has just sold for one hundred thousand pounds?"

I heard my croaky voiced reply.

"My sister."

There were a few gasps and a lot of fingers pointed at me.

"Hey! Cheat!" called Leyton. "Go-karting is OFF. OK?" He was standing next to Niall, as usual. They both had their arms folded and tight, smirking smiles on their faces. I didn't respond. My stomach was tied in knots.

"Cole! Over here!" It was Isla. She was with Mason in the corner of the playground. I quickly walked over.

"Hi," I said, not looking up. I felt all twisted up inside and worried that they were going to say something to make me feel even worse. To be ridiculed by the school bullies was one thing, but if my friends turned their backs on me, that would be unbearable.

"Are you all right?" said Isla.

"My parents hate me," I said, staring at the floor. "I've managed to tell the entire world that I lied about my painting, live on TV. I've had better days to be honest."

"I'm sure they don't hate you," said Isla. "They're just in shock, that's all. They'll be fine when the dust has settled."

I still couldn't look at them in case I started crying.

"What you did was incredibly stupid but ... well, we all make mistakes, don't we?" said Isla.

I felt my insides relax a little. I could cope with anything if Mason and Isla were on my side. But when I risked a glance at Mason he wouldn't look at me.

"And what about you?" I said to him.

"Um ... well..." His face turned pink. "The thing is ... um. My mum and dad heard about what, um ... what you did and they ... don't want me to be mates with you."

"What? Why?!" I said.

Mason shrugged, scuffing his shoe on the floor. I suddenly felt really, really angry. I knew *exactly* why.

"Your parents don't like me, do they?" I spat my words at him. "I saw their faces when I came to your house for your party. I'm not the kind of person they want as your friend. Someone *poor*. That's why I've never been invited round before, isn't it?"

"That's not true!" said Mason, but his cheeks went even redder. "It's nothing to do with you. You saw what they're like with the house! Remember those stupid covers for our feet? And then you knocked over your blackcurrant juice and—"

"You knocked it over!" I said.

"OK, well I knocked it over, but *you* brought it into the dining room in the first place and that's a no-no in our house."

I was about to argue about it being a ridiculous rule when I saw how mortified Mason looked.

"It's not just you, Cole. It's *anyone*. They don't trust *anyone* to come over in case their precious house gets ruined. They're hardly ever there anyway so I don't know what all the fuss is about."

His shoulders hung down low. "And now you've gone and been an idiot, *on national TV*, it makes things even worse. They're just ... weird."

"I think you'll find the word you're looking for is 'snobbish'," I said bitterly. There was an awkward silence as the three of us just stood there. "Forget it," I said. "I'll stay out of your way and then you won't upset Mummy and Daddy, will you?"

I glared at him, trying to provoke him but he just looked really sad. He was silent for a moment, his hands clenched by his sides.

"Do you realize how jealous I am of you?" he suddenly said.

"Jealous?" I said. "Don't be stupid. You've got everything!" I laughed and looked at Isla, but she wasn't smiling.

"OK, so I've got a cinema room and a huge garden and I go on posh holidays, but what do *you* have that I don't, eh, Cole? What do *you* have that I would swap for ANYTHING?"

I shrugged.

"You have a *family*," he said. I frowned. What was he talking about? He had a family too. He carried on. "You have two parents who are actually around to talk to you. Not ones who have to schedule you into their diary. And I'm not joking about that."

I didn't know what to say.

"Think about it. Your family might not have any money, but concentrate on what you *do* have, eh?"

He stared at me for a moment, and then the bell went for registration.

"Listen," said Isla. "I reckon we should go back to the museum after school and see if we can solve any more of the painting." She smiled at us both. "Now you're not busy, how about it, Cole? Get the three of us back together again?"

I looked up at Mason who was staring at the floor.

"OK," I said. The thought of doing something away from the scandal of my lie on TV felt ideal. There was also the slight possibility that we might actually find some treasure at the end of it. Surely Mum and Dad wouldn't be angry at me for that? Was this the chance to make up for all my lies?

"How about you, Mason?" said Isla.

"Yeah, all right," he said, swinging his rucksack over his shoulder.

"Fantastic!" said Isla. "Before we go, I want you to meet me in the drama studio. While you've been busy fooling the world, Cole, I think I've solved the next clue."

She grinned at us and then turned on her heel and headed towards school.

CHAPTER THIRTY-ONE

Mr Taylor Is Very, Very Disappointed

"I am very, very disappointed," said Mr Taylor.

I was back in his office again. Hopefully for the last time.

"I'm disappointed as your headmaster, I'm disappointed on behalf of the staff and I'm disappointed for the entire school."

I stood there listening and stared down at my hands. This time he hadn't offered me a seat.

"The embarrassment you have caused to your family, your school, and ultimately yourself, is quite something."

He shuffled some papers on his desk and looked up at me.

"We have issued a statement of 'no comment' to the press and we won't be changing that at any point in the future. And, unfortunately, Marika Loft has decided to withdraw her offer to finance the refurbishment of the art department."

Great. Now all the teachers would hate me as well. I glanced up at my Mr Taylor. His brow was furrowed as he stared down at the papers in front of him.

"I'm afraid it's down to your parents and Marika's team to try and sort out the mess you now find yourself in."

I wasn't really sure why he'd asked me to go to his office. If it was to make me feel bad then he needn't have bothered. I felt terrible already. And things were about to get much worse.

"I'm afraid some of the members of the press have found your house," he said, clearing his throat. "Apparently, there is quite a crowd gathered outside, waiting for you to get home."

"My house?!" I said. "Why?"

"They want a photo for tomorrow's paper, I guess," said Mr Taylor. "Your mum has asked that you go straight to the museum from school and meet her in the foyer."

"What about Dad and Mabel? Are they OK?" I said.

"Apparently they've gone to stay at your auntie's for a night or two. To escape all the attention."

He must mean Auntie Lynne. She was Mum's sister and, although I hadn't seen her for a year or so, she was really kind.

"Would you like someone to walk to the museum with you?"

I shook my head.

"No, sir. Thank you," I said. Going there with Isla and Mason to try and solve 'An Enigma in Oil' felt like the best distraction right now. I turned to leave and then stopped.

"I'm ... sorry," I said. Mr Taylor didn't look up.

I spent the day trying to dodge the calls of "cheat" and "liar" and worse. After the last bell, Mason and I headed down the corridor to go and meet Isla.

"I'm not taking any notice of what my mum and dad say," said Mason, flushing pink. "Just so you know."

"OK," I said. There was an awkward silence for a moment. "I'm glad you're helping, Mason. What with your superior knowledge of riddle solving and that."

He shoved me on the arm and I grinned.

"I spotted the number on the cabinet when we were looking for the key to get to the canopic jar, didn't I?" he said. "You'd never have got this far without me."

We both laughed.

"At least Isla is helping us, eh?" I said.

As we got closer to the drama studio we could hear a cello.

"That's her," I said to Mason. We waited by the door and listened. Mason didn't say anything. His eyes were wide as the sounds of the cello reverberated in the corridor. He creaked his neck around the door to take a look and the music stopped instantly.

"Well, come in, then!" shouted Isla from inside the room. We both crept in. It felt strange, like we were intruding on something.

Isla was sitting in a chair with her cello between her knees.

"Blimey, Isla," said Mason. "I don't know anything about music, but . . . that was amazing."

Isla grinned. She twiddled a small silver screw at the end of her bow.

"Thanks," she said.

"So, you said you've solved another clue?" I said.

I was looking forward to having something else to think about, other than the really bad day I'd just had.

"OK, are you ready for this?" she said, her eyes wide and sparkling. She reached into her bag and pulled out a large sheet of paper. It was a copy of "An Enigma in Oil". Basil Warrington-Jones's smug face stared out at me.

"I printed this out so that I could work on some ideas when I was at home. The last clue, 'listen to the river', was so intriguing!" she said.

"But what does it mean?" said Mason.

"I'll get to that," she said. "Take a look at the river and tell me, what do you see?"

Mason squinted. "Um . . . water?" he said.

She turned to me.

"Leaves?" I said.

"The leaves are important, yes," she said. "But I think you're both missing the point. This isn't a river at all."

"It isn't?" said Mason. Isla shook her head, then went to her bag again and took out a blank piece of paper and pencil.

"I'm going to draw what I see. These ripples in the water are very important. Can you see there are five of them?"

We watched as she drew five long lines, one under the other.

"And, to me, it looks like those leaves are deliberately positioned on the lines, don't you think?"

Mason nodded and we watched as she drew the leaves as dark circles on to the lines.

"Now, these weeds on one side, they look a bit blurry in this print. I expect it would be much clearer in the original painting. I'm guessing that they are curled into the shape of a treble clef."

She drew a squiggle shape on the left side of the five, straight lines.

"I don't believe it!" said Mason. "It's music! The river is a piece of music!"

He patted her on the shoulder and she glared at him.

"Sorry," he said.

"Isla, that is utterly brilliant. *You* are brilliant!" I said. "There is no way on earth that we'd have spotted that, is there, Mason?" He shook his head.

"When you look at sheets of music as often as I do then it's pretty much staring you in the face," said Isla.

"So now what?" said Mason.

"Now I will play it and we can see if it helps with any

further clues," said Isla, smiling. "I've been waiting so long to do this! I didn't want to try without you two." She grinned at us and then studied the picture. She added two more notes to her sheet of paper, then placed it on to her music stand. There were seven notes in all.

"It's going to be a rough melody," she said, positioning the cello between her knees again and picking up her bow. "I'm not able to tell the duration of the notes or whether they are flats or sharps, but hopefully we'll recognize the tune."

She pressed her fingers on to the strings at the top of the cello and began to play. She played three notes and then stopped. Smiling to herself she started again, this time making each note last longer. When she got to the end she put her bow down.

"Recognize it?" she said. Mason looked as blank as I did.

"It's nice, but no," I said.

"Saint-Saens?" said Isla. "Have you heard of him?" We shook our heads. "Camille Saint-Saens was a French composer. One of his most famous pieces of chamber music was 'The Carnival of the Animals'. Remember it now?"

She had such a big smile on her face that I really, really wanted to say I knew what she was talking about. But I didn't.

"We don't know it, I'm afraid," I said. "Is that what that section of music is called? 'The Carnival of the Animals'?"

"No, 'The Carnival of the Animals' is the name of the whole piece," said Isla. "This little section is just one part of it."

She played the seven notes again as Mason and I listened.

"It's one of the most famous pieces of classical music there is," she said, putting down her bow.

"And what's it called?" I said.

She looked at me and took a long breath as she smiled.

"It's called, 'The Swan'," she said. And just like that, we were back in business.

CHAPTER THIRTY-TWO

The Swan

"The taxidermy birds!" I cried. "Come on. Let's go!"

"What?" said Mason. "What are you talking about?"

I threw my rucksack over my shoulder.

"There's a whole gallery of stuffed birds upstairs in the museum! There must be a swan amongst them somewhere. Are you coming, Isla?"

"Of course!" she said, packing the cello into its case. We waited as she put it into a cupboard and then we headed off. As we walked I told them about what Mr Taylor had said about the journalists at my house.

"They want to get me to say something or get a

photo of me," I said. Isla and Mason were quiet for a bit and then Mason spoke.

"Wow," he said. "So that's how it must feel to be famous."

"It's horrible," I said. "I've never wanted this. I just wanted to help my mum and dad."

"Well, maybe this will be your answer," said Isla, smiling. "If we solve the riddle of 'An Enigma in Oil' then who knows what treasures you'll find!"

When we got to the museum there was a large truck parked outside, with a metal ramp running down to the road. Dr Sabine was directing two men wearing gloves who were carrying a stuffed crocodile.

"Look. They're starting to move things out already," said Mason.

"Before long the whole place will be empty," said Isla. "If we're going to solve the painting then we'll need to be quick."

"Hi, Cole," said Dr Sabine. "Your mum is in the office."

"Thanks, Dr Sabine," I said. "We're going to take a look around first. Before everything goes. Is that OK?"

She smiled. "Of course," she said. We headed to the museum steps.

"What if the birds have gone?" I whispered. "The swan might not even be there any more. It might have been sold."

"Well, there's only one way to find out," said Mason, as we went into the foyer. It was packed with boxes. "Let's go and take a look."

We headed to the back stairs, past the Egyptian section and up to the bird gallery. The sound effects of the seagulls and seascape had been turned off now. It was eerily silent.

"Whoa, creepy," said Isla, looking around. "Do you ever get the feeling you're being watched?" Everywhere you looked there were tiny black beady eyes staring at us from behind glass.

"Right, first one to find the swan gets to keep the treasure. Ready? Steady? Go!" said Mason, running off down the centre of the gallery. Isla giggled and ran in the opposite direction. I headed towards a case full of birds of paradise. I smiled to myself. This was great. I could almost forget about all the trouble I'd caused.

It didn't take long for Mason to call out.

"I've found it!"

Isla and I ran to him.

The stuffed swan was standing amongst some

dry reeds in a cabinet. Its feathers were bright white, but its orange bill looked faded and old. "This is so weird," said Isla, staring at it. "Surely it's better to see an animal in their real habitat, not dead and behind glass?"

"It's a Victorian thing," I said. "Mum said it was fashionable back then." I looked all around the inside of the case, then around the outside. Nothing.

"This is so stupid," said Mason. "What's the point of creating a puzzle that is completely impossible to solve?! It's a waste of time."

Isla took the museum leaflet out of her bag and opened it to the map in the centre. I saw she'd drawn a red circle round the Egyptian gallery where we'd found the canopic jar, and a circle where the model ship was. She took a pen out of her bag and put a circle in the bird gallery.

"What are you doing?" I said.

"Just making a note of where we find each clue," she said, quickly folding up the leaflet and putting it in her pocket. "So, is there anything there?"

"Yes!" said Mason. "There's something around its leg!"

Mason got down on his knees and peered inside the case. Isla and I dived on to the floor to join him.

Around the swan's leg and just above its webbed foot was a piece of paper.

"There's something written on it," said Isla. "I can't read it. Can you?"

I squinted into the gloomy case. I could just make out the tiny handwriting.

"Oh. It only says one word. *Hawaii*."

We all stood back up.

"Any ideas?" I said. Isla and Mason looked blank.

"Hawaii..." said Isla, clearly thinking. "A state of America... What could it mean?"

My head hurt. I didn't know anything about Hawaii.

"I went there once!" said Mason. "Mum and Dad took me. But I was only three."

"Why isn't there more of a clue?" I said. "One word! That's not going to help, is it?"

Isla was pacing around and around.

"It's one clue, but they always draw us back to the picture, don't they? The ship hidden as a rock, the musical notes as ripples in the river... Maybe there is something in the painting that we haven't spotted yet?"

"Cole! What are you doing in here? I said to wait in the foyer." I turned around and saw Mum. Her face looked all crumpled. For a few blissful minutes I had forgotten all about the trouble I was in. Now it hit me in the heart with a dull thud. I'd let my parents down in the most public way possible.

"I'm so sorry about the journalists at our house, Mum," I said, walking towards her. "I truly, truly am."

I thought she was going to give me a hug, but she just sighed.

"Marika's office rang. The sale has been cancelled. She told me they are going to release a statement saying..." Her voice wobbled. "Saying that they had no knowledge that you had submitted someone else's painting, and that you no longer have a contract with the Marika Loft Gallery. The painting has been withdrawn from sale. Fortunately, the highest bidder hadn't paid yet, so that's something to be grateful for. You are very, very lucky that no one is pressing charges against you for fraud."

I nodded. Everything just sounded so serious.

"Declan is bringing Mabel's painting back tomorrow and then, as far as they are concerned, the whole matter will be closed."

"How's Dad?" I asked.

"He's OK. I could do with him being home

though. The new sofa is being delivered tomorrow so I'm going to have to take time off for that."

I'd forgotten all about the new sofa. That was going to cost them more money!

"Can't you cancel it?" I said. "And you can return my trainers!"

Mum's face looked even more strained.

"You can't return the trainers, Cole. You've worn them! And as for the sofa, we rang the shop and we're tied into the contract. We can't get out of it."

I couldn't believe it. We were worse off now than we'd been before the painting had sold!

"But that's stupid," I said. "The shop will have to let you cancel it! You've got to talk to them again."

"Cole, I've already begged them, and they refused!" snapped Mum. "Just leave it, OK? Don't you think you've done enough?"

She took a deep breath and wiped her forehead. This was all my fault.

"Um, sorry to interrupt, Mrs Miller, but we're going to head home. OK, Cole?" said Mason. I'd forgotten he and Isla were there. They must have heard everything.

"Sure," I said.

Isla squeezed my arm.

"Don't worry, we're going to do this," she said quietly. "We've solved three of the clues. That's amazing! Let's try again tomorrow."

I sighed. At the moment, the chance of doing something right in my life felt utterly impossible.

CHAPTER THIRTY-THREE

The Journalists

Mum and I walked home in silence. When we got to our house there was a crowd of people standing on the pavement outside.

"Oh no," said Mum. "I was hoping they'd be gone by now. Come on, Cole. Put your head down."

She placed her arm around my shoulder as we hurried past.

"Mrs Miller! Did you know your son was planning to commit fraud?"

"Are you going to carry on painting, Cole?"

"Does Mabel know her picture sold for all that money?"

"Have you received any of the money from the

sale, Mrs Miller? Have you spent it already?"

"Hey, Cole! How does it feel to have fooled the world?"

We ignored them, rushing into the house and slamming the door behind us. My heart was pounding. We stood in the hallway for a moment, getting our breath back, and then Mum went silently to the kitchen.

"Are you OK, Mum?" I said. She looked at me. Her forehead was all wrinkled and she looked close to tears.

"I'm going to put the kettle on," she said.

The house was unnaturally quiet without Dad and Mabel. I missed them. If it wasn't for me then we'd all be there together. I wouldn't even have minded playing the butterfly game. After dinner I went up to my room, as I had a feeling Mum wanted to be on her own. I lay on my bed and stared at the box of paints that was still sitting in the corner. I could see the tubes of paint were all sticky where Mabel had got her messy hands on them. Everything had gone so wrong. I closed my eyes and willed myself to sleep. It was too early for bed but I didn't want to keep replaying the excruciating moment when my lie was exposed on the five o'clock news. My phone beeped.

I sat up and took a look. It was a group text from Isla and Mason.

Mason: Has anyone had any ideas about Hawaii?

Isla: I've been thinking. Basil's clues are always hidden in a different part of the painting. The jackal in the wood, the rock/ship in the grass and the music in the river.

I quickly flicked to the photograph of the painting on my phone. She was right.

Cole: Yes!

Isla: OK. So, where do you think the next clue might be hidden?

I looked back the picture. There was something completely obvious staring right at me. Or someone.

Cole: Basil Warrington-Jones!

Mason: Him!

Isla: Yes! This puzzle is like completing a word search. The hidden words are never in the same area, are they?

I could see that Mason was typing a reply.

Mason: I can't see anything Hawaiian about him though. . .

I took another look at the painting on my phone and zoomed in on the artist, studying him millimetre by millimetre.

Cole: What about that bunched thing pinned to his jacket? They're feathers, aren't they?

On the lapel of his jacket was a small bunch of something red and yellow.

Mason: Maybe it's something to do with another bird? A bird from Hawaii?

Isla: I doubt it. I don't think the clue would lead you back to the same place in the museum. Let me check the map again.

I jumped off the bed and grabbed the museum leaflet from my school bag. When I sat back down, Isla was already typing.

Isla: Anglo-Saxons, Geology and World Culture are the only areas where we haven't found a clue. I think we know where to look next then?

Mason: World Culture it is! Let's go and look after school tomorrow.

Cole: And Basil said there were four clues so this must be the last one!

I lay back on my bed, my heart not feeling quite as heavy as it had a minute before. There was still a chance that we were actually going to solve 'An Enigma in Oil'. I'd let Mum and Dad down so badly and they were so ashamed of what I'd done. Maybe this was my chance to make it up to them? Maybe solving that painting and finding the treasure could make amends for everything I had done.

CHAPTER THIRTY-FOUR

World Culture

When I left for school the next day, all the journalists had gone. Mum said that she thought they might come back later, but I was just pleased that I could walk to school without anyone shouting at me.

Unfortunately, people were still shouting at me at school. I heard "cheat" at least ten times, but thankfully that was fewer than yesterday.

Mason, Isla and I met at lunchtime and talked about what could be hidden in the World Culture gallery and where it could lead us next.

"I think you're right, Cole: this must be the final clue. We might find the treasure tonight!" said Isla, her eyes glowing.

My heart skipped a beat. I didn't dare think we were that close to solving the whole thing.

After school we practically ran to the museum, and when we got there we headed upstairs and straight to the World Culture gallery. There was a big sign across the door.

GALLERY CLOSED

It was locked.

"Great. Now what?" I said.

"Hang on," said Isla. "There's someone in there."

I peeked through the glass door and saw the back of Dr Sabine. She was typing on to a laptop which was balanced on top of a low cabinet. I knocked and she turned around and came over to unlock the door.

"Dr Sabine! We're looking for something! Is there anything in there that has feathers? We are so, so close, we just need to look for one more thing!"

Dr Sabine blinked at me.

"Whoa, slow down, Cole. What is it you're after?" she said.

I looked at Mason and Isla.

"I think we should tell her what we're doing," said Isla.

Dr Sabine looked between the three of us.

"Go on then," she said. "I'm all ears."

"We're going to solve 'An Enigma in Oil'," said Isla, a great grin on her face.

"Oh, are you?" said Dr Sabine, looking amused. "You do realize it hasn't been solved in over a hundred years, don't you?"

"Yes, but we're really close!" said Mason. "We just need to take a look in this gallery." Dr Sabine looked at her watch. She clearly thought we were wasting her time.

"That's great, but I really need to get on," she said.

"We won't be long," I said.

"I'm sorry," said Dr Sabine. "I've just got too much work to do. Your mum had to go home early today because your new sofa is arriving."

My heart sank. I'd forgotten about that.

"Look, I really commend you for what you're trying to do." She glanced at me. "But the museum needs to be emptied ready for closure and I have to get everything packed up and out of here as soon as possible."

She went to close the door.

"Dr Sabine," said Isla, stepping forward, her voice loud and clear. "We have solved three clues from 'An Enigma in Oil' so far. I am *convinced* that we are about to solve the fourth and final clue and we know that the clue is somewhere in the room behind you."

I saw Isla's throat go up and down as she swallowed. Dr Sabine frowned.

"I'm sorry? Did you say you've solved *three* clues?"

"Yes!" I said.

"B-but . . . how?"

"Isla did the hardest bits, to be honest," said Mason, pointing at Isla who blushed.

"It was all of us really," she said. "But we are sure that the last clue has something to do with feathers and might be in this very room. We really won't be long, I promise."

Dr Sabine sighed.

"OK," she said, opening the door wide. "You've got five minutes and then I'll need you to leave."

"Thank you, Dr Sabine," said Isla, smiling brightly.

"And if it's feathers you're after then you'd better check the cabinet by the fire exit," she said, nodding towards a dark corner. She turned and walked back to her laptop.

We all rushed over to the cabinet, which had a long, dark cloak hanging on a mannequin inside.

"I thought she said it had something to do with feathers," said Mason. "This isn't going to help!"

Isla stood closer and read the sign.

"Hang on!" she said. "Listen to this … it's from *Hawaii!*" She turned and grinned at us. My stomach did a triple somersault. Isla read aloud.

"Such cloaks were worn only by the highest chiefs, as a sign of their semi-divine rank." She stopped to take a closer look at the cloak. "It's incredible. And there's more, listen: *A cloak of this size has been estimated to contain … 450,000 feathers.*"

I stepped closer and saw that the cloak was in fact made of tiny feathers, all woven together, the same colour as those in Basil's lapel.

"It's amazing!" said Mason.

"And highly valuable," said Dr Sabine, coming over to join us. "This is an incredibly rare piece. And before long it'll be shipped off to its new owner, probably in a private collection where hardly anyone will get to see it."

"That's so sad," said Isla.

"It truly is, Isla," said Dr Sabine. "Right, have you found want you wanted?"

"Can we just have three more minutes, Dr Sabine?" I said.

"Three minutes and then you'll have to leave," she said, turning to go. "Oh, and by the way, I'd love to know more about how you've managed to solve the painting so far. Do tell me all about it when I'm not so busy, won't you?"

"We will," grinned Isla. As soon as Dr Sabine had left we gathered around the cloak and looked all around the case.

"Hang on, there's something pinned just inside the hemline," said Mason. "It's in another language. Isla?"

She leant forward.

"It's Latin!" She said. "'It says ... *responsum oculos spectat...*'"

She took out her phone.

"Let's see if I can translate it online," she said, tapping the screen. We waited and then she slowly looked back up at us.

"It says, *The answer looks you in the eyes.*"

"What on earth does that mean?" I said. I could almost see Isla's brain whirring.

"It's looking us in the eyes. It's like he's saying the answer is staring us in the face."

"I don't get it," said Mason. "The clues are in the

painting and we *are* looking at them. He's stating the obvious! Of course the answer is staring us in the face! But how can we solve it just by looking at it?"

We made our way out of the World Culture collection and into the corridor. Isla had taken the museum leaflet out of her bag and she placed a red circle where we'd found the last clue, on the Hawaiian cloak. She studied it for a moment, then placed the map against the wall and drew lines between where each clue had been hidden. It made a very lopsided square, some edges much longer than others.

"Hang on," I said, grabbing the pen and leaflet. "How about if you draw a line diagonally? So, from here ... to here..."

I drew the red pen from the top left corner to the bottom right corner, and then from the top right corner to the bottom left. In the centre of the square was a large X. For a second it reminded me of the vapour trails in my painting, 'A Sky in Blue'.

"Oh, wow. X marks the spot!" said Mason.

"That's it!" said Isla. "That's where the treasure is hidden. Let's go!"

The X on the map was hovering in a space towards the front of the museum. As we headed there I tried to think of where it could be. Behind the information desk? Or did one of the steps have a hidden panel? When we got there, we crowded around the map and checked the position again.

I banged my foot on the first few stairs, testing to see if they sounded hollow. Nothing. I looked all around and then it dawned on me. All of our running around the different areas of the museum trying to find the treasure had been a wild goose chase, set by an artist with mischief on his mind. But I'd cracked it, I'd beaten Basil: I knew *exactly* where the treasure was.

"I've got it!" I said. "It's the painting! Of course! The answer is staring you in the face and the X has led us back to the painting. The treasure must be hidden somewhere *inside* the painting, in the frame, in the back, something like that!"

"That's genius," Mason said, shaking his head.

"Oh, wow!" said Isla. "To hide the treasure *inside* the actual picture. Brilliant!"

We were all quiet for a moment as we realized what we had done.

We'd done it.

We'd actually solved 'An Enigma in Oil'.

But when we turned to look up at the painting all that was there was a bare section of wall.

"It's gone!" said Isla.

CHAPTER THIRTY-FIVE

A Surprise Visit

We found Dr Sabine and bombarded her with questions about the whereabouts of the painting.

"I'm sorry," said Dr Sabine. "A lot of our artefacts have been sold now, including 'An Enigma in Oil'. It's being transported to its new home as we speak."

"But who's bought it?" said Isla. "Can we go and see it?"

Dr Sabine shook her head.

"I'm afraid it's gone to a private collector. It won't be on public show any more."

"Who?! Who's bought it?" said Mason.

"That information is confidential, I'm afraid," she said. "Now, off you go. I'm sorry but I've given you long enough and I've still got a lot of work to be getting on with."

I felt sick. That was it. The painting was gone, along with its treasure. We turned away and made our way back through the museum.

"I don't believe it. We've come so far! How can it be sold? How?" I said. I could feel tears prickling in my eyes. I tried not to blink in case they escaped.

"I'm so sorry, Cole," said Isla, placing her hand on my arm. "We were so close. It's not fair."

"I just wanted to help my mum and dad," I said, letting the tears come at the memory of their disappointed faces. "I wanted to say sorry for everything that I've done, the mess I got us all into."

I wiped my eyes.

"They were so excited when I sold the painting. It was like all their problems had vanished. And then I made everything a million times worse. I've ruined *everything*."

We walked through the foyer and I looked up again at the blank space on the wall. I sighed as we headed outside into the daylight.

"This was my one chance to put things right," I said. "I'd find the treasure and show Mum and Dad that I *could* do something to help our family. And now that's all gone wrong too."

"Come on," said Isla. "Let's go home."

We made our way down the museum steps and as I stopped to wipe my face on my sleeve someone tapped me on the shoulder. I turned around. It was Declan, Marika's PA, and he was actually smiling at us.

"What are you doing here?" I asked, hoping he wouldn't be too angry with me.

"I've just been to your house, actually. To return the painting. Your *sister's* painting."

I felt myself blush.

"I'm sorry, Declan," I said, hanging my head. "I'm sorry I've wasted so much of your time."

Declan looked at me carefully for a moment, then patted my shoulder. "I think you've been punished enough, don't you, Cole? It's time for all of us to move on. Speaking of which, I'm actually heading back to London now. I've been overseeing a purchase that Marika has made from the museum."

"Marika has bought something from the museum?" asked Mason.

"Yep," said Declan, checking his phone and putting it in the inside pocket of his jacket. "Marika has an incredible amount of art from all around the world for her own private collection. Although I think she's purchased this one for purely sentimental reasons."

"Art?" said Isla. "She's bought a picture?"

Declan frowned. "Yes, she has actually."

My heart started to pound. "She's bought 'An Enigma in Oil' hasn't she?" I asked.

"As a matter of fact she has," he said. "That painting made a big impression on her when she was a child. She used to come and view it with her father, intrigued by the riddle within. But I'd appreciate it if you kept that to yourselves. Right, I'd better get back to London..."

I grabbed his elbow.

"Declan, please. We need your help," I said. "We are trying to solve the mystery of the painting and we're so nearly there, but we need to see it close up. Can you help us?"

He rubbed his head. "That's a bit tricky, I'm afraid. It's about to go to London and—"

"It's still here?!" said Mason. "In the museum?"

Declan looked a bit panicked. "Not *in* the museum exactly..."

"Then where is it?" I said. "*Please*, Declan. It'll only take five minutes, I promise!"

Declan sighed as he thought about it.

"Hang on," he said, taking his phone out of his pocket. "I'll see if I can stop them."

The three of us stared at each other. Isla gripped my arm.

"It's going to be all right, Cole," she said. "This isn't over yet. I just know it."

Declan walked away as he spoke on the phone and we all watched him in silence. Eventually he turned back, putting his phone away.

"The van is going to park around the corner. You've got five minutes to take a look and then it *has* to go, OK? You've caused Marika enough trouble, Cole, I don't want any more delays here."

We nodded.

"OK," said Declan, looking a bit fed up. "Let's go."

We followed him down the road and into a side street. As we turned down the road a black van pulled up and parked. Declan said something to the driver and then he went to the back doors and opened them.

"Quick, turn on your phone torches," said Mason.

"Five minutes," said Declan again and we climbed up into the van.

It took a while for my eyes to adjust to the darkness and then I saw that the painting was strapped to the left side, covered by a huge, grey blanket. Isla quickly reached for the buckle and undid it. The painting began to fall forward and the three of us quickly reached up to stop it.

"Place it back gently," said Isla. "Rest it against the side."

When the painting was propped up, we stood there for a moment. I suddenly felt really nervous. What if we were wrong? What if there was nothing there?

"Come on then," said Isla. "Let's get the blanket off and take a look."

We carefully pulled the blanket down and I gulped as I came face to face with Basil Warrington-Jones. He was so close I could see the small lines around his dark eyes.

"Hello, Basil," I whispered. "We've come to claim your treasure, if that's OK with you?"

Basil smiled back at me.

"Look at the river," said Mason, shining the torch from his phone along the water. "It glistens!"

He was right. The light from his torch caught flecks of white paint on the canvas which made it look like the water was actually flowing and rippling.

"We need to get around the back," I said.

"Let's edge it away from the side and you can squeeze behind it, Cole," said Isla. "Ready?"

"Ready," I said. Isla and Mason stood in position at each end of the painting. They held on to the frame and carefully edged it away from the side of the van using tiny movements.

"It's so heavy. I bet it's full of gold!" said Mason. "Or diamonds!"

"Sshhh," said Isla. "Keep quiet!"

She was right. If Declan saw what we were doing he'd tell us to get out of the van immediately. I had to hurry.

"Is there enough room now?" said Mason, his voice sounding strained.

"I think so," I said. I squeezed behind the giant painting. "Edge it forward a bit more, I can't see."

They moved the painting a few more centimetres away from the side of the van and then I had some space to take a proper look.

"Can you see anything?" said Isla.

"Nothing," I said, moving the light from my phone all around. "It's covered by some kind of thick material." But I could see some small metal tacks holding the fabric in place.

"It looks like it's nailed to the back," I said.

"Can't you just rip it off?" said Mason.

"No, Mason. I can't just rip it off. It's fastened tight! I'll need a knife or something to cut my way in," I said. My torch trembled a little. There had to be something here, there just *had* to. I followed the light along the edge of the frame and paused.

"I think you'd better come out now," said Isla, her voice strained. "We can't hold it for much longer."

"Just a few more seconds!" I said and pointed my torch across the back of the fabric.

"What on earth are you doing? I said you could look at it, not move it!" The van swayed as Declan climbed through the back doors. My torch wobbled and the light lit up an area in the bottom left of the fabric. It was bulging.

"Cole! Get out from behind there. I can't believe you've—"

"Wait! I've found something!" I cried. "Just wait! Please!"

I crouched down and felt along the fabric where the folds had been. It was a pocket! A small, rectangular pocket that had been stitched on to the cloth. I lifted the flap and put my hand inside and my fingers felt something made of paper. I pulled it out. There was a handwritten note wrapped around some banknotes.

"It's money!" I called, my heart racing. "I've found the treasure and it's money!"

I came out from behind the painting and held out the notes. Mason and Isla gently placed the painting back against the side of the van. Declan looked livid.

"How much is there?" asked Isla, her voice squeaking with excitement.

"I don't know. It's all old notes," I said.

"What are you doing?!" said Declan, carefully covering the painting back up. "This is a precious painting and I did not give you permission to move it!"

"We've solved 'An Enigma in Oil'," said Isla. "Look! Cole has found the prize."

I held on to the roll of banknotes.

"Let me see," said Declan. I took off the handwritten message and gave him the notes. He quickly counted them. "There are ten very old five-pound notes."

"Fifty pounds?" I said. "Is that it?!"

He nodded.

"That would have been a huge sum back in the early 1900s," said Isla quietly. "It would have been the equivalent of thousands in today's money."

"But that's no good to me now, is it?" I cried. "I

thought there was going to be enough to help us. But it's just a few worthless banknotes!"

I turned and stared right at Basil Warrington-Jones.

"Look at him! He's just a stupid artist who thought it would be fun to make me look a fool," I said. "Well, Basil. Congratulations. You succeeded."

Mason cleared his throat.

"I'm so sorry, Cole," he said. "What does the note say?"

I swallowed hard, unfolded the piece of paper and began to read.

Congratulations!

You have found my prize and I applaud your ingenuity with all of my heart.

Take this money and do with it what you wish.

But remember, the greatest thing you can possess in this life is love.

And that comes for free.

Basil Warrington-Jones 11th May, 1909.

I scrunched the note up in my hand and dropped it on the floor.

"That's it then. Basil won after all," I said. I turned

to Declan. "Thank you for letting us take a look at the painting, Declan. Sorry we wasted your time."

And I jumped down from the van and ran all the way home.

CHAPTER THIRTY-SIX

Dad and Mabel Return

As I walked home my phone beeped. I had two text messages.

Isla: I'm so sorry, Cole. You tried so hard.

Mason: Bad luck, mate. At least we solved the mystery though, eh? No one's managed that before!

I let myself in just as Mum was walking into the hallway. She gave me a weak smile.

"Declan dropped your sister's painting off earlier," she said. "He said that Marika is keeping a low profile to avoid all the bad publicity. Everyone is laughing at her for being fooled by a twelve-year-old, apparently."

Whatever I said would probably just make things worse, so I kept quiet.

"As we've got some hot water for a change I'm going to have a bath." She turned away and I watched as she walked slowly up the stairs. I so wanted to come home and tell her some good news: that we'd cracked the clues in the painting, found the treasure and our money worries were over – for real this time. But I couldn't. Basil Warrington-Jones had truly had the last laugh.

Mum hadn't mentioned the new sofa but I could smell it before I went into the lounge. It looked ridiculous in our scruffy room. I sat down and the soft cushion dipped gently. Leaning against it was a black cloth bag. I picked it up, my stomach churning. Mabel's painting was inside. The painting that had caused all my problems. I pulled the strings tight, then ran upstairs and threw it under my bed out of sight.

Dad and Mabel arrived back from Auntie Lynne's while I was in bed. Dad poked his head into my room, even though my light was off.

"Hey, Cole," he whispered around the door. "How are you doing?"

I pretended to be asleep, but he came in anyway.

"Mum is just putting Mabel to bed. She fell asleep on the train on the way home, but she's really looking forward to seeing you in the morning."

I rolled on to my back and tucked my chin down into my chest.

"I'm so sorry, Dad," I said, trying not to cry. "For everything."

He frowned.

"Cole, let me tell you something," he said. "Are you listening?"

I nodded. He took a deep breath.

"I was thinking on our way home. All of us are a bit like trains really, aren't we?" I stared at him. Where was he going with this?

"You can be chuffing along on your track without a care in the world. The sun is shining and everything is wonderful and your journey is smooth and straight forward."

I stared at my duvet as I listened.

"But sometimes your track might veer off in a completely different direction," he said. "Now, this part of the journey might be tricky. The sun could go behind a dark cloud and before you know it, you're faced with a really tough hill to climb. You might get

303

to the top of that hill, and then feel scared or out of control as you hurtle downwards, not knowing which direction the bend is going to twist and turn."

I thought about Mabel's painting, the auction, being on TV and everything that had gone on over the past few weeks. It had certainly felt scary and a bit like being on a runaway train. Dad paused for a moment.

"But eventually, that terrifying journey will lead you back on to the right track. Before you know it you'll be steaming along again and the sun will come out from behind that stormy cloud. The scary bits will all be behind you."

I sniffed.

"And when will that happen?" I said. "When will I be back on the normal track?"

Dad smiled.

"I think you're coming around the corner right now, don't you?" he said. "But the important thing to remember is this. All of it matters. The easy, straight track, the climb up the hill, the scary descent; it's all just a part of your journey."

I blinked at him as I thought about it. It had been a very stressful time, there was no doubt about that. My track had definitely veered off in a terrifying direction, but I'd also discovered a lot along the way. For one, I'd made some amazing friends. Mason and Isla had really stood beside me, even when everyone else was laughing. And as for Mum and Dad, I don't think Mason's parents would have been as kind or understanding if it had been him whose lies had snowballed out of control and who had ended up on national television embarrassing their entire family. All in all, I was actually incredibly lucky.

"Thanks, Dad," I said. And then I sat up and gave him a big hug.

CHAPTER THIRTY-SEVEN

Back on the News

I woke up the next morning to hear Dad's mobile phone ringing. It stopped and then our home phone began to ring. My stomach turned over. The sound reminded me of when we were on the six o'clock news and everyone found out that it was really Mabel's painting that had sold at auction. What had happened now? I curled up under my duvet and kept my eyes shut. Whatever was going on I didn't want to know about it.

About twenty minutes later I heard my bedroom door open.

"Cole!" said a voice. I felt a hand thump on to my legs.

"Go away, Mabel," I mumbled, pulling the duvet

higher over my head. The doorbell rang and I heard it open and close and then the clamour of lots of voices.

"Cole! Can you come down for a minute please?" called Mum up the stairs.

I groaned.

"Come on, Cole!" said Mabel, banging me on the legs again. Now what? I slowly got out of bed and made my way downstairs as Mabel bumped her way behind me on her bottom. Mum and Dad were standing in the front room, waiting for me. Declan was sitting on our new sofa and beside him was Marika.

"Oh. It's you!" I said, blinking at her. She smiled softly.

"It is. Hello, Cole."

My legs felt shaky so I sat down. What had I done wrong now? I didn't think I could cope with anything else. Mabel ran into the room and hid behind Mum's legs.

"Oh, so this must be Mabel!" said Marika, smiling at my little sister, who stared back shyly. "Get in touch when you're a bit older and we might be able to do a deal for your paintings, don't you think?"

Everyone laughed and I relaxed a little. They all seemed different. They seemed … happy. I saw that

Declan was holding a bundle of old banknotes. It was the money that had been hidden behind the canvas of 'An Enigma in Oil'. In his other hand he had the note, smoothed out from where I'd scrunched it up.

"Declan said that you solved the painting, Cole," said Mum. "Why didn't you tell us?"

I shrugged.

"There wasn't anything there, just some old money that's pretty worthless," I said. "It was a waste of time."

Marika shook her head. "But it hasn't been, Cole. What you have done is incredible."

I looked at her and she flashed her wide, bright smile.

"You were right about the treasure," said Declan. "There's not a huge amount of value in these old notes. Some collector might pay a few hundred for them, that's all."

"So ... what's incredible?" I said.

"It's the publicity," said Marika, her eyes twinkling. "That painting has baffled experts for over a hundred years. And now you and your friends have solved it! That's a wonderful achievement."

Mum grinned at me, and tears pricked my eyes when I saw how proud she was.

"It's in the papers already," said Declan. "Look!"

THE BOY WHO FOOLED THE WORLD SOLVES MYSTERY PAINTING.

Cole Miller, the 12-year-old boy who fooled the Marika Loft Gallery and hundreds of bidders by selling a picture that was actually painted by his THREE-year-old sister for £100,000, has SOLVED the mystery of 'An Enigma in Oil'. The artist, Basil Warrington-Jones, donated the painting to the Crowther Museum in 1909. He declared it contained a "treasure map" which led to a substantial reward, causing hundreds of people to try and solve the riddle.

The answers to the mysterious painting have remained hidden, until now. Cole Miller and his two friends made it their mission to find the treasure and they succeeded where many have failed. The reward, a few old banknotes, is of little value, but the news that the picture has finally been solved is expected to spark a new interest in Basil Warrington-Jones, and the museum itself. There are unconfirmed reports that the museum's closure has now been put on hold so that the general public can visit and see the painting, and the clues that led to the treasure, for themselves.

I put the paper down and looked up.

"The museum's not closing?" I said.

Mum shook her head. "Dr Sabine rang first thing. They're going to keep us open for at least another six months!"

"But that's brilliant!" I said. "You can keep your job!" The relief and beaming smile on Mum's face was the best thing I'd ever seen.

"I've had lots of requests for an interview," Declan said to me. "How do you feel about that?"

I shook my head.

"No. No journalists and no TV crews this time, thank you," I said. "If they want to find out more then they'll just have to go to the museum."

Mum laughed and gave me a huge hug.

"We're planning a big exhibition about Basil Warrington-Jones and the painting. We are going to highlight the clues in the areas that you found so that everyone can find out more about them. You'll have to tell me how you did it!"

I nodded, then I thought of something.

"But Marika owns the painting now," I said, turning to her. "The exhibition won't be complete if it's not on display in the museum."

"I was only buying the painting to give it a safe

home," Marika said. "Its true home is in the museum. I've cancelled the sale."

"But what about all the other things that have been sold?" I said. I thought about the men carrying out the stuffed crocodile.

"The museum has hundreds of other items in storage which they are going to put on display, isn't that right, Jenny?" said Dad.

Mum nodded.

"Yes, we can't wait to show all the treasures that no one has seen for decades. We are going to plan some really big reveals for some of them too!"

Declan passed me the pile of banknotes. "I believe these belong to you, Cole," he said. "You could try contacting an expert and see if you can sell them?"

I shook my head. "I think they should go back to the museum," I said. "You could use them as part of the 'Enigma in Oil' exhibition, Mum?"

Mum smiled.

"That sounds like a fantastic idea," she said.

CHAPTER THIRTY-EIGHT

Mabel Miller

A few days later Mum and Dr Sabine appeared on the local news telling everyone just how wonderful their museum was. Dr Sabine took the jackal-headed canopic jar with her and explained what it was and how Basil Warrington-Jones had used it as part of his treasure hunt. Mum asked if I was sure I didn't want to go on TV with them, but I said no. I had had enough publicity to last a lifetime.

Mum was brilliant on television. She didn't look nervous at all; she just talked about her job and how important the museum was for the local community.

"There's not many places where you can see a real mammoth hair, right up close," she'd said. The presenter laughed, thinking she was making it up, but Mum went on to insist that it was true. Their little local museum had a real hair from a real mammoth on display in one of the glass cabinets in the grand gallery. I decided I'd make sure I went back to take a look at that for myself. It sounded amazing.

When I got home from school, Dad was just getting his coat on to go out.

"Ah, there you are," he said nervously. "I'm off now, Cole. Mum will be back at the usual time."

"OK, Dad. Good luck," I said. "You'll be fantastic."

Dad smiled, but he looked scared. He had a job interview. When we'd been on TV – the day that Mabel had told the world that the painting was hers – Dad had mentioned to the presenter that he used to be a music roadie. The manager of the local theatre had seen him and got in touch. They were looking for a stagehand to work in the evenings when they had shows and they liked the fact that he had experience with sound and lighting.

Dad took a deep breath as he opened the front door.

"Remember, you're just approaching a bend in your track, Dad, that's all," I said. Dad smiled at me and then walked out with his head held high. I closed the door behind him. I had a good feeling about this job.

My little sister was spinning around beside me.

"Mabel have a biscuit, Cole?" she said, as soon as Dad had gone.

"I've got something even better for you, Mabel," I said. "Follow me."

I headed upstairs and she padded up behind me. I went into my room, knelt on the carpet and reached under my bed, pulling out the black cloth bag that Declan had returned on the day we solved 'An Enigma in Oil'. Mabel's eyes widened when I opened the bag.

"Mabel's painting!" she said, reaching out her arms. She sat cross-legged and put it on her lap and gazed at the bright colours. "That's Mabel and that's Cole," she said, pointing at the two rectangular blobs.

"Yep, that's us," I said. "But there's something you need to do, Mabel. To show that the painting is really yours."

I took a brush and tube of blue paint from the art box that was still sitting in the corner of my room. I painted over the "C" that I'd put there, and then I chose a bright yellow paint from the box and dabbed the brush into it.

"I was once told that it's very important to sign your work," I said. My sister stared at me, her eyes wide. "I'll help you, shall I? We can put an 'M' for Mabel just there."

Mabel grinned and grabbed the brush and I helped to guide her hand as we painted the wonky letter.

We both admired the painting as Mabel held it up.

"'Catch' by Mabel Miller," I said out loud. "That's all your work! You're so clever."

Not long ago, this painting was worth a hundred thousand pounds. It seemed impossible to believe it now. Mabel sighed and dropped the painting on to the floor.

"Cole play the butterfly game?" she said.

I smiled at her.

"OK, Mabel," I said. "Let's play."

Lisa Thompson's Favourite Hoaxes from History

There have been some particularly fascinating hoaxes throughout history. Some funny, some a bit … gruesome, but all incredibly clever. Here are some of my favourites!

Spaghetti Trees:

I'm not a big fan of April Fool's Day and I've never really understood the desire to make other people feel silly, but this must be one of the best April Fool's deceptions ever. In 1957 the BBC TV news show Panorama orchestrated a pretty spectacular hoax on their viewers. During the programme, they transmitted a three-minute film of a family in Switzerland harvesting spaghetti from their "spaghetti trees". Pasta was not an everyday food item back then, and of the eight million viewers that saw the black-and-white footage, many of them were fooled. The next day hundreds of people rang the

BBC, asking how they could grow their own spaghetti trees. Brilliant!

Fiji Mermaid:

In 1842, the showman P.T. Barnum exhibited the "Fiji Mermaid" in his American Museum in New York. He advertised the creature using drawings of beautiful mermaids with long, flowing hair, but this mermaid was anything but. It was, in fact, made from the head and body of a small monkey sewn on to the tail of a fish, and it was believed to have been made by a Japanese fisherman. In Barnum's autobiography he described it exactly as it looked: "an ugly, dried-up, black-looking, and diminutive specimen ... its arms thrown up, giving it the appearance of having died in great agony."

Han van Meegeren:

Han van Meegeren was a classically trained Dutch artist living in the 1930s. His work was criticised for being unoriginal, and as a way of getting revenge on his critics, he decided to create a "new" work by an artist called Johannes Vermeer – an old master who lived in the seventeenth century. Van Meegeren was very clever and made sure he used a genuine seventeenth century canvas and pigments, and then he added a substance called Bakelite which, when baked in the oven, made the paint dry very hard and crack, giving the impression that the picture was hundreds of years old. He fooled everybody, and over the next few years he created six more "Vermeers" as well as paintings by other Dutch masters. Van Meegeren was eventually arrested for treason shortly after World War II when it came to light that he had sold a painting to a Nazi leader. His only defence was to admit that the artwork had been forged. The story was big news at the time, and Van Meegeren became known as the world's greatest art forger of the twentieth century. By this point he had accumulated the equivalent of $30 million!

Platypus:

And then we have the rather confusing hoax that wasn't a hoax... The duck-billed platypus. This creature baffled European scientists when they first encountered its preserved body in 1799. It had a duck-like bill, a body like an otter and a tail like a beaver.

It was no surprise that they thought that, just like the Fiji Mermaid, the creature had been stitched together as a hoax.

Pierre Brassau – the monkey artist

In 1964, four paintings by a previously unknown French artist, Pierre Brassau, were exhibited in Sweden. The praise for the paintings from art critics and journalists was pretty unanimous. One critic said, "Pierre is an artist who performs with the delicacy of a ballet dancer." Just one found the work disagreeable, saying, "Only an ape could have done this." They were correct. Pierre Brassau was in fact a four-year-old West African chimpanzee called Peter from a zoo in Sweden. The hoax has been thought up by a journalist to put art critics to the test. Could these "experts" tell the difference between modern art and paintings by a monkey? I wonder what Marika Loft would have made of it all?

It seemed that Peter quite enjoyed painting and he always had a bunch of bananas beside him while he worked. Apparently, he would eat as many as nine during a ten-minute art session.

1917 Cottingley Fairies

One of my favourite hoaxes was actually instigated by children. Elsie Wright (16) and Frances Griffiths (9) lived in Cottingley, Bradford, in the early part of the twentieth century. The two girls often played by a stream at Elsie's house, telling their parents they went there to see the fairies. To prove it, Elsie borrowed her father's camera and after the photograph was developed, it appeared to show Frances smiling at the lens while four fairies danced in front of her. The girls went on to produce four more "fairy" photographs, which caused a great deal of interest from the public, scientists, and even from the Sherlock Holmes author, Sir Arthur Conan Doyle, who was convinced that the photographs were evidence of psychic phenomena.

Just like the excitement waned over the treasure hunt hidden in the painting 'An Enigma in Oil' in my book, interest in the Cottingley Fairies declined after 1921 and it wasn't until the 1980s that Elsie and Frances finally admitted that they were fakes. Imagine keeping a secret like that for all of those years? They said that the fairies were, in fact, cardboard cut-outs – something that the scientific investigations failed to spot. However, the story doesn't end quite there because Frances still maintained that the fifth and final photo was completely genuine… So maybe it wasn't entirely a hoax after all?

Don't miss …

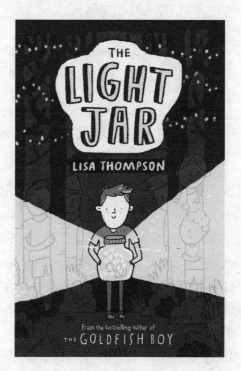

In the dead of night, Nate and his mum
run away to a tumbledown cottage
in the middle of a dark forest.

Read an extract now. . .

THE COTTAGE

"Why can't we stay with Grandma?" I asked Mum.

We sat in the car as the rain hammered down and stared at the dirty grey cottage that was lit up by Mum's headlights. The image I'd pictured of a holiday we'd once had in a cosy, quaint cottage completely vanished. About thirty years ago this house was probably quite pretty, with its white walls and roses around the door. Now the walls were the colour of a muddy puddle and it looked like it was slowly being swallowed by blankets of thick, dark ivy. I didn't recognize this place at all. The dirt track that we turned down from the main road must have been at least two kilometres long. Mum was right: this was really off the radar.

I didn't want to go inside. I wanted us to turn around right now and go somewhere else.

"I thought it might be a bit untidy ... but this?" said Mum, and she leaned forward and rested her chin on the steering wheel. "This is terrible! How has it been left to get in such a state?"

"We should go, Mum. I don't like it here. Let's go to Grandma's."

She ignored me again. Mum and Grandma had a big argument and hadn't spoken since Granddad's funeral, which was months ago now.

"Wait here, Nate, and I'll go and find the key. This weather is probably making it look worse than it is. I bet it's not so bad inside."

She pulled her cardigan tightly around her neck then got out into the torrential rain and waded through the weeds to the porch door. She ran her hand along one edge of the roof and then went round to the other side out of sight.

I stared through one of the cottage windows. There was a faint yellow light coming from the corner of a room. The car window steamed up and I rubbed at it with my sleeve and squinted into the gloom but the glow had gone. I must have imagined it.

Mum appeared holding a large key in her hand.

She tugged at the ivy on the porch and then fumbled with the lock and began to push at the door with her shoulder. She had to keep stopping to wipe the rain out of her eyes but after ten more shoves the door began to inch open and she squeezed through, tugging at it from the inside before beckoning me to join her.

I stared up at the ramshackle old house. Rainwater poured from a hole in the gutter above one of the windows, which made it look like it was crying. Mum waved me towards her again. She was splattered with mud and her hair was plastered to her face and she was gripping the side of the door as if it was helping to hold her up.

"I don't want to be here," I said under my breath, and then I picked up my rucksack and opened the car door.

Mum flicked a light switch in the lounge and a bare bulb dangling in the middle of the ceiling spluttered into life, giving off a feeble glow.

"Look, Nate. We have light!" said Mum, but I didn't answer.

She made her way back to the front door.

"You wait here and I'll get our bags."

I wanted to run after her, shut the stupid, awkward

door and get straight back into the car. The house looked like it hadn't been cleaned for about a hundred years and there was a smell like something was rotting. In front of the stone-cold fireplace was a sofa that was probably quite squishy and comfortable fifty years ago, but now it looked like it had had its insides sucked out. Something moved in the gloom and I jumped. Sitting on one of the arms of the sofa was a scruffy brown chicken. It cocked its head at me, and blinked with a dark, round eye.

"What are *you* doing here?" yelled Mum, walking in and waving our two bags madly. "Get out! Go on. Shoo! This isn't your home!"

The chicken gave a squawk and then did a half-hearted flutter up on to the windowsill and jumped through a square of broken glass. It huddled outside on the ledge, sheltering from the freezing rain as much as it could.

The sofa was covered in lots of grey lumps and it was only when I stepped closer I realized it was chicken poo, which probably explained the smell.

"We can't stay here, Mum. Look at the sofa, it's disgusting."

Mum didn't turn around. She just stood in front of the broken window, staring at the bird.

"There's droppings everywhere. And there are probably rats and all sorts crawling around. And we haven't even been upstairs yet. Where are we going to sleep? We can't stay here – we've *got* to go somewhere else!"

The chicken sank its head into its body as far as it could, its eyes barely open as the rain and wind blew, ruffling its feathers. Mum's fingers were clenched by her sides. She didn't turn round.

"Mum? I said we've got to go! Let's just get in the car and drive to Grandma's, OK?"

She was saying something quietly to herself. Her eyes were wide and fixed on the chicken and she was shivering, her clothes soaked through.

"She just wanted a home, Nate. She didn't mean to make a mess. She just wanted a little home to shelter in."

Tears were running down her face but she wasn't making any crying noises. I put my arm around her and patted her hand.

"It's OK, Mum. It's just a chicken."

I looked out into the night-time, at the pounding rain and the silhouettes of dark trees.

"I don't know what I'm doing, Nate. I don't know what's right or wrong any more," said Mum, her voice shaking. "You know that feeling when you think the ground is going to split in two and you could just fall and keep on falling for ever? Like Alice does when she tumbles through that rabbit hole into Wonderland? But rather than floating down and landing at the bottom you just keep on going. Down and down and down."

I shook my head as she looked at me. I didn't know the feeling she was talking about. I was scared. I hadn't seen her like this before. It was as though her body was there but her insides were missing, just like the sofa. She blinked and her eyes seemed to come back into focus again and she quickly wiped her wet cheeks and patted me on the arm.

"I'm just tired, Nate, that's all."

She peeled off her wet cardigan and hung it over an old wooden chair.

I held tightly to my rucksack at my shoulder. I didn't want to go back but I didn't want to stay here either. Mum headed towards a doorway which must have led to the kitchen.

"I'm going to see what I can find to patch the hole in the window. Why don't you go on upstairs and see how the beds look? We'll both feel better after some sleep, I'm sure."

She turned away and I stood there for a moment, thinking what to do. Then I headed back towards the front door and stood at the bottom of the stairs. I pressed the light switch and the bulb at the top flickered. It looked very dark up there. I took a deep breath and held on to the banister. Each step groaned as I walked but, amazingly, I managed to get to the top without crashing through to the floor. At the top of the stairs was a bathroom with an old-fashioned toilet where you had to pull on a chain to flush it. There was a fat spider sitting in the middle of the bath and I tapped the side and watched as it scurried away down the plughole.